84 in Brooklyn

PHIL NOVA

ISBN: 978-0-578-72397-6
Five Borough Publishing
New York

CHAPTER 1

Brooklyn, New York. June 1984.

Angelo Manigritto and his friends just graduated high school and had been spending most of their days on Coney Island beach, drinking beer, smoking weed, and checking out the bikinis.

But on the last day of June, the temperature dropped to below seventy and it rained all day, so Angelo stayed in, mostly eating and sleeping.

His bedroom was messier than his mother would have liked it to be, but cleaner than any of his friends kept their rooms. A crucifix hung over his bed, above the headboard. His father had hung it there when Angelo just an infant in a crib and it had hung there ever since.

Angelo's mother didn't mind him decorating his own room, but she wasn't crazy about his latest choice of décor—posters hung with thumbtacks. Posters of Conan, Jason Voorhees, and Daisy Duke. A few old Yankees pennants hung on the back of his door. They were old and tattered but he refused the throw them away because his father had given them to him when he was just a boy.

That night while he showered, Angelo's mother, a typical chubby Italian woman in a housedress, pressed his clothes with so much starch they could have stood by themselves. He wore a pair of pleated slacks and a long-sleeve button-down shirt that had more colors than the disco ball at the nightclub he was preparing for.

He had told his mother she didn't need to cook, and for once, she actually listened. He gave her some money to order Chinese food even though he knew she would save most of it to play cards with her friends.

It didn't make sense to take his black '79 Lincoln Mark V to the car wash in the rain, so he had even more free time to kill while waiting for his sixteen-year-old sister,

Gianna, to finish getting dressed. He had promised to drop her off at her friend's house about twenty blocks away before going to meet his friends.

Gianna had been a short chubby little girl, but once she hit puberty, she sprouted up and lost all the baby fat. She was now skinny and very pretty.

"You didn't bring an umbrella?" Asked Angelo.

"No. You have one?"

"I forgot mine at school about a month ago."

She got out of Angelo's car and hurried to her friend's front door.

The block was a quiet tree-lined residential street with two-story semi-attached brick houses on both sides.

Angelo waited to be sure Gianna's little friend was home before taking off. When the girl opened the door dressed like Madonna, he noticed how much she'd developed since the last time he'd seen her, especially the hips and breasts. He quickly removed the thoughts from his mind. Now that he was over eighteen, sixteen was jailbait. He wasn't scared of going to jail, he knew he'd be going there one day, but it wouldn't be for banging a minor. No matter how hot she was.

Gianna waved to Angelo then entered her friend's house.

Angelo drove to Bay Ridge to meet his friend, Frank Freij, whose nickname was Frankie Arms. Frank got into Angelo's car and pulled out a fat joint. "Appetizer, anyone?"

"Don't mind if I do." Angelo pushed in the cigarette lighter to warm it up.

When the lighter was ready, it popped out and Frank lit the joint.

Angelo said, "Be careful with those ashes."

"I know. I know." He took a deep hit.

Angelo scanned the radio stations and stopped when he heard Caribbean Queen.

They arrived at the Vegas Diner on 86th Street in Bensonhurst, which had opened two years earlier and was famous for its disco fries—steak cut fries with melted mozzarella and gravy.

Most kids their age didn't venture out of their own neighborhood very often, but Angelo and his friends weren't like most kids. They went wherever they wanted to go.

Angelo parked in the open lot, then he and Frank entered the one-story fieldstone faced building.

The Americana Diner was closer to Frank's house and the club, but they liked the food better at the Vegas, and it also seemed more upscale.

Inside, bright lights reflected off highly polished furniture, glass, and mirrors while Sinatra songs played in the background. Most of the tables were occupied while waiters, waitresses, and bus boys zipped back and forth.

Their best friends, Mikey Potatoes and Patty the Mick were already there waiting for them in the smoking section. Angelo had met Frank when they were on the football team together at Lafayette High School, but he'd known Mike and Pat since they were little kids at PS-97. The kids in grammar school said Mikey always smelled of potatoes and they taunted him so long with the nickname that he began to like it and it stuck. Pat's nickname was less original. They called him a Mick because he was Irish.

Mike and Pat were both short and thin with no facial hair. Mike had darker skin and hair while Pat was pale with dirty blond hair and one eye that was always half-closed.

Pat lived with his grandmother, who hadn't been cooking much since her hip replacement, and while Mike's mother was alive and well, she couldn't be bothered to cook, so Pat and Mike spent a lot of time eating out.

Angelo usually ate at home before going to the club, but because he had promised to drop off his sister, it was still too early to go out, so he decided to kill some time eating at the diner with his friends.

Of course, he could have gone to eat at Frank's house, but Frank's mother, who was of Italian descent, but couldn't cook Italian food for shit, usually cooked dishes that came from Frank's father's home country of Lebanon, and Angelo wasn't in the mood to be experimental.

They squeezed into the booth with their friends.

Mike said, "Nice cologne."

Angelo and Frank laughed.

Pat said, "I told you that was some good weed. We just picked up eight more pounds."

A middle-aged waitress flirted with the boys while taking their orders.

Angelo's friends laughed and made comments when Angelo ordered just a salad. His mother had fed him a big lunch earlier and he didn't want to take the chance of having to take a shit in the nightclub, so he forced down his salad while eying Frank's T-bone steak.

After dinner, they all enjoyed a cigarette, then paid their bill and left.

The sun had gone down and the rain had lightened up. The cool air cut through to Angelo's bones. He had his leather jacket in the car but didn't want to wrinkle his perfectly pressed shirt, so he suffered.

They drove in two cars back to Bay Ridge and smoked more weed on the way. They also took a small bump of coke to get their heart rates up.

As Frank wiped the powder from his nose, his eyes bulged and he held his stomach. "I think I gotta take a shit."

Angelo laughed. "I bet you wish you had the salad now." He pulled up alongside the parked cars and waved the valet over. He gave the kid a generous tip then he and Frank hurried into the club to avoid getting soaked by the rain. Angelo liked to tip ahead of time so the driver would take extra care of his car.

Pastel's nightclub was packed, but the owner, as well as the made men who frequented there, all knew who

Angelo's uncle was, so he always got in. The legal drinking age in most of America was 18, but in New York, it was 21. Most clubs in Brooklyn and other parts of the city let people slide if they were close enough.

Bright spinning disco balls overhead, and flashing lights under the clear dance floor, illuminated the otherwise dark nightclub as people danced their asses off.

Disco may have been dead in most of America, but not in Brooklyn.

The DJ also played the occasional top 40 hit, which was usually new wave or freestyle, but he mostly played disco.

Mike and Pat made their rounds selling weed while Angelo and Frank downed a couple drinks at the bar then approached the two sluttiest looking chicks they could find. Frank could dance to anything, but Angelo only went for the slow dances. He never felt comfortable shaking his ass. Regardless, they both ended up getting blowjobs in the bathroom.

CHAPTER 2

Angelo's little sister, Gianna, was also giving someone a blowjob.

Leo, a 19-year-old drug dealer with a baby face and a pencil-thin beard and mustache, relaxed on the sofa at Gianna's friend's house while Gianna knelt down in front of him.

Her little friend and another guy sat on the sofa next to them. Gianna's friend had already sucked her guy dry and was now loading her glass stem with a fresh rock. She moved the lighter in circular motions around the glass, slowly bubbling up the crack while inhaling.

A Run DMC cassette played loudly from a boom box while unfinished cigarettes burned in the ashtray.

The girl's parents were away in Atlantic City for the weekend and Gianna had lied to her mother and Angelo about her friend's parents taking them to the movies.

Gianna's head was still ringing from her last hit but she wanted more. She lifted her head momentarily to get a hit from the stem before going back down. The rush hit her instantly. Her brain swelled as she listened to what sounded like helicopters inside her skull. Leo put his hand on her head and pushed her back down.

After a few minutes, the paranoia hit. Gianna lifted her head and began to look around, grinding her teeth. Leo must have sensed it because he pulled her up onto the sofa, pulled up her little skirt, and pulled her panties to the side. It only took a few minutes for him to finish. He didn't have a condom on and he didn't try to pull it out, he blew his load inside her, and then he zipped up and lit a cigarette.

Before walking out the door, Leo left a large rock on the table. "This should keep you girls busy for a while.

You want more . . . come by the hood . . . the fellas would be very happy to meet you."

Leo asked his friend, "Where do you want me to drop you off?"

"Why can't I go with you?"

"You know my cousins don't want no one going with me on these runs."

The two girls were too busy smoking to pay attention to Leo and his friend as they left.

Every hit seemed to fade away faster than the last. Always chasing that first hit.

They tried to ration what they had, but it was futile. It burned up quickly.

CHAPTER 3

Agent Cortes, a short, stout, forty-four-year-old DEA agent with a thick mustache was back on the job for the first time in two months. Twenty-five years of two-pack-a-day cigarette smoking had finally taken its toll. He had recently been diagnosed with lung cancer and had surgery to remove the infected tissue.

He was going crazy at home, especially now that he couldn't smoke, so being back in the field felt as if he'd just been let out of a cage. He was ready to jump right in and go after his white whale, the Ghost of 3rd Avenue.

Of course, he didn't believe in Ghosts literally. The 3rd Avenue Ghosts was the name of a gang who sold crack on the streets of Brooklyn's Sunset Park neighborhood. Anyone who tried to move into their territory was mysteriously killed or never seen again. No one had ever seen or heard anything when the murders happened, so people began calling the killer *the Ghost.* The gang changed their name from the 3rd Avenue Boyz to the 3rd Avenue Ghosts and embraced the Ghost story when they learned that it spread fear. None of the police informants nor any of the street people in the area had ever actually met anyone nicknamed the Ghost.

After either killing or scaring away their competition, the Ghosts began expanding their operation farther down and into Park Slope. The cops knew it was their crack because instead of vials, which were beginning to gain popularity everywhere else in the city, they still used tiny baggies . . . theirs had a picture of a Ghost printed on them and their crack was always the most powerful.

Agent Cortes had spent his first four years with the DEA in Miami and Los Angeles. He was very successful, so when the crack epidemic hit in 1982, his superiors said that his experience and expertise was needed in America's biggest city, New York.

He began working in Manhattan at first, where he had been very effective, but when he heard about the 3rd Avenue Ghost killings in Brooklyn last year, he requested the case.

Outside of Leo's six-story apartment building, Agent Cortes sat in the driver's seat of his government-issued gray van with tinted windows while the windshield wipers pulsed.

Sitting in the passenger seat of the van was Cortes' 28-year-old partner, Agent Wicker, a tall husky white farm boy from Montana with brown hair and a full beard. Wicker looked more like a lumberjack than an officer of the law, but that was usually to his advantage.

On a tip from a paid informant, the DEA agents were waiting for Leo to get home, and when he got there, they called the NYPD to provide them with a pair of cops in a patrol car.

He hadn't lived in Texas since joining the army in 1958, but Agent Cortes still spoke with an accent. On the radio, he told the NYPD dispatcher, "Tell them to wait on 6th Avenue and then pull him over when he turns off his block."

Agent Wicker asked, "And what if they can't find a reason to pull him over?"

"Don't worry. The NYPD knows how to manufacture excuses."

"But—"

Agent Cortes interrupted. "What? Would you rather see the streets flooded with more crack?"

Agent Wicker didn't answer.

Cortes knew that Wicker had been an MP for five years in the marines, so he couldn't help being a stickler for the rules. He'd patiently teach the kid that out here in the streets, sometimes the rules had to be bent. Occasionally even broken.

Sitting there, watching Leo's building, and waiting for him to come back out, Agent Cortes was dying for a cigarette. But the notion quickly passed when he thought about the surgery he'd just undergone eight weeks earlier.

Leo lived in the building on the corner, but he parked his little red BMW with a dented right fender in an open lot down the block, which was a one-way street.

After at least thirty minutes, Leo came outside with an umbrella over his head. He had something else in his other hand as he hurried to his car.

Agent Cortes picked up the radio and said, "Tell those boys he's coming their way. Let me know when he's in custody." They waited a few minutes as Leo drove down his block and then stopped at the stop sign. Leo's car hesitated and Agent Cortes began to worry that he had made them or that he didn't have anything on him.

Finally, a black cab pulled up behind Leo and beeped.

Leo made the turn onto 6th Avenue.

Agent Cortes started the van and rolled forward with the lights off in case anyone inside Leo's building was watching them. When he arrived at the intersection, he turned the lights on and made the turn.

The uniformed cops had their sirens on and Leo's car pulled over, checking his driver's license.

Cortes passed them then slowed down on the next block, pulling over to the side and watching through the rearview mirror. Between the rain and the flashing sirens, he could barely make out what was going on.

One cop had Leo out of his car, patting him down while the other cop seemed to be searching the car. After a few minutes, the two cops were cuffing Leo and placing him into the back of their patrol car.

The DEA agents got a call on the radio. A woman's voice said, "They have him in custody."

Agent Cortes asked, "What did he have on him?"

The female voice replied, "Blow . . . and a lot of it."

"Excellent." Agent Cortes said, "Tell them to follow us."

"Copy."

The sirens turned off and the cops began moving forward.

Agent Wicker asked, "Aren't we going to meet them at their precinct?"

"Not just yet, young buck." Agent Cortes drove a few blocks while the cops followed them.

They passed houses, apartment buildings, and a school before finally arriving in an area made up of construction supply houses. All the buildings had their steel gates rolled down and both sides of the street were lined with graffiti-covered trucks that were parked for the night.

Agent Cortes slowed down. He could tell by his partner's face that he didn't approve as he stepped out of the van and approached the cops. "Bring him here."

The rain had finally stopped, leaving behind a cool fresh breeze.

As the cops pulled Leo from their car, he struggled and yelled, "Yo bro! What the fuck you doing? This shit is illegal. I want my lawyer. Yo!"

Agent Cortes opened the van's back door, "Throw him in there."

The cops hesitated.

Cortes assured them, "Don't worry. I'm not a violent man."

The cops pushed Leo into the back of the van and then Cortes climbed in with him and closed the back door. He was definitely too weak to fight if he had to, but he knew he was safe, not only because Leo's hands were cuffed behind him, but because of his hulking corn-fed partner, who was still in the van.

Leo looked around at all the surveillance equipment. "This is illegal. My lawyer will have your badges. You won't get away with this."

"Shut up and listen for a minute." Agent Cortes felt like giving Leo a good slap across the face and then enjoying a good cigarette, but he couldn't do either. "We're not cops . . . and we don't give a shit about you. We want the Ghost."

Leo chuckled. "Then you should be looking for a haunted house."

Agent Cortes pulled up the sleeve of Leo's T-shirt revealing a tattoo that read, *3AV,* and was surrounded by roses. "I know you're with the Ghosts."

"I want my lawyer."

Agent Cortes once again noticed the lack of approval on his partner's face, but he wasn't ready to cut the kid loose just yet. "You want money? We can get you money. Enough money for you to get far away from here and live like a king."

"Lawyer."

"If you won't negotiate then you're going to jail. That's a lot of coke. You'll be going away for a long time."

Once again, Leo said, "Lawyer."

Agent Cortes wanted a cigarette even more now. He realized he was wasting his time. "Last chance . . . no? Fuck you, then." He opened the back door and spoke to the two cops who were standing there, "Take this little dirtbag to jail. You picked him up for running the stop sign then smelled marijuana, which gave you probable cause to search his car. Then you called us, we got in our van and followed you to the precinct."

"Got it." The first cop took Leo out of the van.

Agent Cortes glared at the second cop who was silent. "You got that, officer?"

CHAPTER 4

After the girls had smoked the last of their crack, Gianna searched her friend's living room carpet just in case any tiny particles may have fallen. Every time she picked up a piece of lint, her friend was there asking what she had.

Eventually, Gianna began to remember her friend going into the kitchen earlier. She was sure she'd hid something in there. "I know you have more in the kitchen."

"What?"

"I saw you go in there before."

"To drink some water."

Gianna thought about it for a moment, then exclaimed, "You're lying."

"Fuck you."

"I know you're holding out on me, bitch." Gianna moved toward the kitchen.

Her friend followed her in.

Gianna began opening drawers and cabinets and pulling things apart. When her friend tried to stop her, Gianna scratched her face. They hit each other until falling down, then they wrestled on the linoleum floor.

Her little friend grabbed one of the knives that Gianna had dropped and swung it.

Gianna moved out of the way then raced out the back door.

It took a few seconds to get her bearings, then she snuck along the concrete driveway between the two houses until reaching the sidewalk. Her high was gone but her paranoia was just beginning. She needed another hit.

The residential street was quiet, but then she turned the corner and proceeded down the avenue, which was still busy with people going to restaurants and doing last minute shopping. They moved out of Gianna's way when they saw her bulging eyes and dripping make-up. She glanced at her reflection in a window and tried to straighten her messy hair with her hand.

Wanting to get away from all the lights and people, Gianna headed down another quiet street lined with houses.

In her head, everything on the wet sidewalk looked like money or more crack . . . but every time she went for it, it was something else: cigarette butts, scraps of paper, gum that people had spit out.

She continued like that for a couple of hours, moving slowly toward her house, and even though it began to drizzle again, Gianna still stopped to pick up everything she saw.

CHAPTER 5

Pastel's night club would be open until 5 AM, but Angelo was starved after only eating a salad for dinner. He convinced his friends to get out of there and go for something to eat.

Outside, other than people from the club, most of the area was quiet. The rain was gone but it left behind a thick fog.

Angelo gave the valet his tickets and another tip, then he lit up a joint and passed it around to his friends while discussing where they were going to eat.

Mike blew the smoke out of his lungs, coughed, and said, "I feel like Chinese food."

Pat took the joint and replied, "Fuck Chinese food. I want breakfast." He took a deep drag then handed it to Angelo.

Angelo hit the joint, and while holding in the smoke, he grunted, "I could go for breakfast."

Frank said, "I'm down for breakfast, too. But, let's go the Del Rio this time."

Pat said, "They have the same menu as the Vegas."

"They're owned by the same people." Added Angelo.

Mike said, "Yeah, because you like that chubby chick that works at the Del Rio."

Pat asked, "What is it with you and those big girls?"

Frank replied, "I like a girl with some boom boom in the back."

"Boom Boom?" Angelo laughed. "That girl's ass could cause an earthquake. I've seen you in the locker room. I don't think you can do much damage."

Frank replied, "Don't worry about it. It gets bigger than what you seen in the locker room."

They all laughed as they finished up the joint and their cars arrived.

As Angelo drove, he was so buzzed from the drinks, the weed, and the coke that he had to squint to see through the steamy night air. He turned off the radio so he could concentrate better as he drove. "You know . . . the Americana is a lot closer. Now I gotta drive you all the way back."

"I'll take a cab back."

It took a while to get from Pastel's to King's Highway, but at least the parking lot had a few good spots left.

The Del Rio diner was almost identical to the Vegas, just a little bit older, and instead of a flat black roof, the Del Rio had a red tile roof.

Angelo retrieved a loaded 9mm Beretta from under the seat and slipped it under his waistband behind his back, a trick he learned from watching Magnum PI. He then pulled his now wrinkled shirt over it and covered that with his leather jacket.

Frank asked, "Expecting trouble?"

"Always." Angelo put a cigarette in his mouth, lit it, then got out of his Lincoln.

Mike and Pat got out of Mike's ten-year-old Monte Carlo, then, the four of them entered the building.

The diner was busy for 3 AM, but not so crowded they couldn't find a seat. This time, instead of squeezing into a booth, they sat at a table and enjoyed the extra elbow room.

When a cute skinny waitress approached, Angelo noticed the look of disappointment on Frank's face. Despite Frank being much more handsome than Angelo, he was the best wingman. It always seemed that girls traveled in pairs, and for some reason, it was always a hot one with a big one. Frank always went for the big one, leaving Angelo with no competition.

The waitress must have been new, because she was obviously nervous. Frank, Mike, and Pat ordered bacon and eggs. Angelo was so hungry, and he couldn't make up his mind, so he ordered two breakfasts: Eggs Benedict and pancakes.

While they ate, Angelo spotted the chubby waitress working in the non-smoking section. She had long silky black hair and the face of a perfect angel, but she definitely took up two seats in the subway.

After they finished eating, Frank stood. "I'm going in." He stepped away from the table and almost bumped into a sexy older woman coming from the other direction. He apologized before going on his way.

As the woman passed the table, Pat said, "Excuse me, Miss. You dropped something."

When she turned around to look, Pat said, "My heart."

Angelo and Mike laughed, shaking their heads.

The woman smiled. "That was cute." She showed him the rock on her left hand. "But I'm a married woman."

Two big men who liked like construction workers sitting at the next table turned their heads.

One of them stood and approached the woman. "These clowns bothering you, babe?"

"Nobody's bothering me. Let's go back to the table."

Everyone looked when Mike raised his voice. "Who the fuck you calling clowns?"

Angelo chuckled because Mike was the smallest guy in the whole diner but he was the loudest.

The big man boomed, "You . . . you little fucking punk! Get up and do something about it!"

Mike slammed his fists on the table and then stood, "Come on!"

The other big man stood next to his friend and the woman who was sitting next to him hurried to the counter with the check and some cash in her hand.

Angelo lit a cigarette. "You want to fight? I'll throw both of you jerkoffs a beating if that's what yous want. But we just finished our meals . . . and we'd like to digest first."

Frank was on his way back over there by that point. He stood behind the two men, obviously ready to pounce.

The second man chuckled. "Digest? What are you going swimming? Or are you just talking shit, you fucking pussy?"

Angelo retrieved the pistol from his waistband and laid it on the table. He then blew a puff of smoke into their faces and said. "As soon as this cigarette is done . . . we can take it outside."

The two men had already noticed Frank standing behind them, now they both had their eyes on the gun on the table.

"Let's go." The woman nudged the big man. "I'm fucking serious. Let's go."

The two big men glared at the four defiant eighteen-year-olds, but they left, and they kept their mouths shut.

They could hear the woman scolding him on their way out the door. "You gotta start a fight everywhere we go?"

CHAPTER 6

By the time Gianna got to Avenue U she was no longer high but feeling the miserable after-effects of the crack. Her jaw was sore from all the grinding and her body felt as if she'd just run a marathon.

The sunlight was just becoming visible through the fog.

Standing in front of her red-brick two-story detached house, Gianna tried to compose herself.

She wasn't sure if she'd lost her key or if she'd forgotten it, but she had no choice now but to ring the bell and hope that her brother wasn't home yet.

Her mother answered the door cursing in Italian with an occasional choice English word thrown into the mix.

"I wanted to call you, Ma, but my friend's phone wasn't working."

She wasn't sure if her mother had even heard her because she just kept cursing.

Gianna went into the bathroom, closed the door, then hated herself when she saw how disgusting she looked in the mirror. A tear ran down her face, but it wasn't noticeable among the streaked make up.

CHAPTER 7

Angelo entered his house while trying not to wake up his mother and sister, but when he got through the door, he found his mother wide-awake, waiting for him in the living room. She had the same expression on her face that she'd had when he got into trouble as a child. "What's wrong, Ma? Why you up so early?"

"Your little sister just got home a half-hour ago. I tried calling her beeper so many times. And you should see what she looked like . . . like she rolled around in the filthy gutter before coming home." She then spit out her usual array of Italian curse words.

"Where is she?"

"She's in bed . . . now."

"I'll talk to her when I wake up. I got a bad headache, Ma. Just let me get some sleep."

She didn't answer. She just sat there with steam coming out of her ears.

Angelo leaned in, kissed her on the cheek, then headed upstairs to his bedroom.

He didn't want his little sister out all night either, but he didn't find it to be the worst thing in the world, especially if he was just getting home himself. He'd give Gianna a good talking to in the morning, and by that time, he knew his mother would have had enough time to calm down.

At that moment, the only thing he cared about was a handful of aspirin and his bed.

CHAPTER 8

After a long and peaceful slumber, Angelo stuck his head out the window and took a couple puffs from a joint.

The hot sun was in the middle of the sky.

He then lit up a cigarette and placed it in the ashtray to burn out the smell of the weed while he went down the hall and brushed his teeth.

It was late afternoon by the time he was showered and ready for an early Sunday dinner.

When Angelo entered the kitchen, his mother ranted, "She's still sleeping. I tried to wake her up a few times but she don't move. Who sleeps all day? She might as well be dead. *Morte*."

"I'll get her." Angelo left the kitchen and went upstairs to his sister's room. He knocked twice before opening the door and going inside.

The stuffed animals that usually sat on a shelf were all on the floor and Gianna's drawers were all opened with the clothes half pulled out.

Her hair was greasy and knotted while her makeup was smeared all over her face and pillow. Angelo knew their mother was going to go crazy when she saw what had happened to Gianna's new set of white sheets.

Gianna was obviously dehydrated by the why she slapped her lips with her tongue in between bouts of snoring so loud and erratic that it sounded as if she was going to suffocate to death.

Angelo had never seen her like that. He assumed she drank more than she could handle and he hoped that she had learned her lesson.

He pushed her, "Gianna. Get up. It's dinnertime already."

She opened her eyes then closed them again and whined, "I don't wanna get up."

"You been sleeping all day. Get up and get yourself together."

She whined again, "But I—"

Angelo yelled, "Get up!"

She got out of her bed and then gave him the evil eye as she made her way down the hall to the bathroom.

Angelo went downstairs and into the kitchen where his mother was stirring the sauce.

Italian ceramic tiles covered the kitchen floors and all of the appliances and cookware were top of the line.

"She's up. She's in the bathroom."

His mother replied, "It's about time."

Angelo inhaled the aroma. "Is that crab sauce?"

"Yeah. They had a good deal down the fish market."

"You need help with anything?"

"Of course not."

"I'm going for a cigarette in the living room."

The rest of the house had polished marble floors with high-end Victorian furniture in every room. Most of the furniture had been around since before their father had died, but their mother kept everything looking as if it had just come off the showroom floor. The walls were covered with family pictures as well as religious pictures.

Gianna came downstairs.

Angelo said, "You better apologize to her."

"For what?"

"For staying out all night and not calling."

"You were out all night."

"But I have my beeper on me . . . and if someone pages me . . . I call them back. And besides . . . I'm a man."

"How is that fair?"

"It's not. But it's life. Get used to it."

They went into the kitchen and sat at the table.

Their mother served them.

Gianna muttered, "I'm sorry for staying out all night."

Their mother replied, "*Bugiarda.*"

"I apologize and she calls me a liar?"

Angelo protested, "Come on, Ma. She said she's sorry. What do you want?"

Their mother took a deep breath, then surrendered. "Okay. I forgive you."

After eating their meal in complete silence, Gianna stood and said, "I'll be home by eleven."

Her mother replied, "What? Are you kidding me? You're not going nowhere. It's bad enough you have to go to summer school because of your grades, you're not going to fuck that up, too."

"But I promised my friend we'd study together. You want me to fail tomorrow's test?"

"You can study by yourself. Here at home."

"But I promised her."

"I don't want you seeing that little *puttana* anymore after she had you out all night like that."

"This is a different friend. And I promised."

Angelo finally said something, "Let her go study until nine. That's a fair compromise."

His mother said, "Just go then." She stood and began clearing the table.

Gianna left the kitchen.

Angelo cracked the window and lit up a cigarette while his mother washed the dishes.

Later, when his mother went next door to play cards with her friends, Angelo smoked a fat joint and then popped a copy of the recently released on home video, Scarface, into the VCR and watched it on the thirty-two-inch living room television.

CHAPTER 9

By the time Gianna had gotten home that the morning, she told herself she would never touch crack again, but by the time she woke up to her mother and her brother breaking chops, she was ready to get high.

There was no friend she was going to study with, instead, she called Leo from a payphone. Leo didn't answer, so she called his cousin, Juan Carlo Arroyo. They had never met, but she had spoken to him on the phone before so he knew who she was and what she wanted. Leo had even built her up on the phone, telling his cousin how beautiful she was.

Juan Carlo told her to take a cab to his basement hideout on 4th Avenue, and that he'd pay for it when she got there.

She went to a car service just a few blocks from her house and then sat in the back of the car while ignoring the old driver who kept ogling her through his rearview mirror. Traffic on Bay Ridge Parkway was heavy and her stomach was twisted in knots. She wished she could get there faster and get that first hit.

When the car made the turn going down 4th Avenue and went under the overpass, the neighborhood changed to Sunset Park. Stores and restaurants occupied both sides of the wide busy avenue.

They turned the corner and passed a crowd of people sitting on a stoop with Salsa music blaring from an oversized boom-box. Then they continued up the block passing old three-story limestone row houses that were all in need of a facelift.

The driver slowed down in front of the last house before the building on the corner and said, "This is it."

At first, she didn't see anyone and she worried that she had gone to the wrong place, then she saw Juan Carlo coming up a short set of stairs from the building next door. He was twenty-two-years-old and light-skinned with a thin mustache, thick black hair, and a thin face. Gianna knew that Juan Carlo and his brother, Gerard, ran the gang. She knew because Leo was drunk one night bragging to her about it. But she also knew enough to keep her mouth shut.

Juan Carlo paid the driver, then like a gentleman, he opened the door for Gianna and led her toward the building on the corner, which housed a busy tire shop.

Downstairs, inside the musty basement, a few chairs and a torn-up sofa sat around a makeshift table with milk crates and plywood. Empty beer cans and bottles were everywhere as well as ashtrays full of cigarette butts and weed roaches. Freestyle music played loudly from a tall speaker that looked like it belonged at a concert.

Gianna felt disgusted when she first entered and looked around, but once she got that first hit of crack into her lungs, nothing mattered except the next hit . . . and the next.

Juan Carlo got to fuck Gianna first since he was the senior member of the gang.

The other guys drank beers and waited their turn while making jokes.

Gianna wasn't even sure how many guys fucked her or if any of them used condoms, they just kept moving her into different positions and pounding her, but one thing she did know, there was enough crack to keep her with a steady high.

She had no idea how long she had been there, but they finally told her she had to go. Juan Carlo gave her money for a cab, but Gianna didn't want to go. They had to forcibly remove her from the filthy little basement apartment and push her out onto the sidewalk. The tire shop had long been closed by that time and when she kept banging on the basement door, the upstairs neighbors yelled out their window for her to stop banging. Juan Carlo had no choice but to have two of his friends drive her home.

After they dropped her off on her block, rather than go home, Gianna spent another couple hours wandering the dark streets of her own neighborhood until her high finally faded away, then she went back home, once again feeling like shit.

CHAPTER 10

After watching Scarface on tape last night, Angelo had gone upstairs to his bedroom and paged his sister before lying down. She was late, but their mother wasn't home yet, so he was going to tell her to get her ass home before she got into more trouble.

While waiting for his sister to call, he opened the latest Flex magazine and read an article by Arnold Schwarzenegger on his training for the latest Conan movie.

Angelo didn't remember what time he had fallen asleep, but he knew it was three o'clock in the morning when he woke up to his mother yelling that his sister still wasn't home and wasn't answering her pages again.

Now that he had just started a steroid cycle, the last thing he needed was to be aggravated in the middle of the night. "I paged her, too. Maybe her battery died. There's nothing we can do about it right now. Just let me get some sleep. I'll deal with her in the morning." He closed his eyes. He didn't hear his mother leave the room, but he certainly heard her slam the door.

He wasn't sure how long it had been, but he was still tired when he awoke to the sound of his mother yelling again. He got up and stepped out of his room.

Down the hall, she yelled at Gianna, who once again looked a mess. But this time Angelo knew she wasn't just out drinking. He'd seen those bulging eyes and grinding jaw plenty of times. She was coked up. He said, "Go downstairs, Ma."

"What?"

He felt bad to have to raise his voice to his mother, but this time it was necessary. "Go downstairs!"

When their mother was out of sight, Angelo slapped Gianna across the face. "You think I don't know what the fuck you've been doing?"

"You're not my father!" she stormed into her room and slammed the door.

CHAPTER 11

Agent Cortes spent about thirty minutes coughing and spitting when he woke up. He could barely put down a cup of coffee. He knew he could have easily gotten more time off from the DEA even though the doctor had already given him the okay to go back to work. He wasn't ready to lay down and die just yet, not until his case was solved and the Ghost was no longer a myth, rather just another dirtbag rotting in jail.

When Cortes had moved to New York two years earlier, he expected to continue moving around to different cities with the DEA, so he rented a small house in suburban New Jersey rather than trying to buy one. An apartment would have been big enough, but the rents were high and most apartment buildings didn't allow pets. Cortes had one cat, but it was so high strung that it spent most of its days hiding and only came out late at night. He knew the cat was still alive because the food he put out every morning was gone by the time he got home at night and the litter box always needed changing.

Cortes had always been on the messy side. It drove his ex-wife crazy. He still had half-unpacked boxes from two years earlier and every inch of the little rental house that wasn't covered with dirty clothes was covered in dust. He kept telling himself to hire a cleaning woman, but never got around to doing it.

The air conditioner in the window was off, but Cortes still felt cold and weak. He almost considered skipping his shower but changed his mind when he thought about that cute new junior agent at the office. Obviously, he wasn't in any shape to think about young women, but that didn't mean he had to get lazy and stinky.

He showered quickly and got dressed, and despite the fact that he was off to an early start, he still got stuck in traffic going into New York.

The sun was barely visible on the horizon through the mist and he could hear the ships in the harbor talking to each other with their foghorns.

Cortes took the Holland Tunnel into Manhattan then circled around the downtown area on the West Side Highway. After passing the Twin Towers and other massive skyscrapers, he came back up the east side and then finally crossed into Brooklyn on the Williamsburg Bridge, passing the old Domino Sugar Factory.

Although the 3rd Avenue Ghosts had only been known to sell in Sunset Park and Park Slope, a couple of crackheads in Williamsburg had just been arrested a few hours earlier and they had quite a few Ghost branded crack baggies on them.

Agent Cortes had a feeling that if left unchecked, the Ghost gang would eventually be supplying all of Brooklyn. And he didn't trust the NYPD not to take kickbacks.

When he arrived at the ancient Williamsburg precinct, Agent Cortes spoke with the arresting officer and then with the two crackheads in separate interview rooms. They both told so many lies neither of them could keep their story straight. Plus, they were both twisted from being cracked up, probably for weeks.

Cortes yelled and threatened them both with jail time, but the crackheads were obviously veterans and they paid him no mind. They just kept manufacturing stories. Cortes' last resort would have been violence, which he knew from experience never worked on drug-addicts. He could have gotten them to talk by giving them some crack and a stem, but that wasn't going to happen there in the precinct, so finally, he gave up.

When he went downstairs, he found Agent Wicker with a cup of coffee in his hand.

Wicker asked, "What are we doing here?"

"They arrested a couple of dirtbags with Ghost crack on them last night."

Detective Zaragoza, a thin, handsome plainclothes narcotics detective with a dark complexion, entered and stopped when he saw the two DEA agents.

They had all met once before at a joint DEA-NYPD seminar about the rising crack epidemic and Cortes and Zaragoza had spoken on the phone a few times since then.

The three men shook hands and exchanged pleasantries.

Agent Cortes said, "Looks like we found you just in time."

Detective Zaragoza replied, "I'll say. I was just getting ready to clock out, and I won't be back in New York until Saturday night."

"I heard." Agent Cortes fought his urges once again when he saw a young cop outside smoking a cigarette. He turned back to the detective and said, "Your captain says you're taking the kids to Disneyland."

"Disneyworld. California is too long of a flight for me."

Agent Wicker added, "I took my kids there last year. It was expensive. But they loved it."

Detective Zaragoza changed the subject. "So . . . I heard about those Ghost baggies. Did they say anything?"

"Lies upon lies. They won't talk."

The detective said, "It's an isolated incident. They probably bought the stuff up there and then brought it back here. They both live in the projects a few blocks away. We know them well."

Agent Cortes agreed, "You're probably right. Get out of here. Enjoy your vacation."

They all shook hands again and then Detective Zaragoza entered the precinct while the two DEA agents returned to their cars. The rising sun finally began to cut through the fog.

CHAPTER 12

Juan Carlo's brother, Gerard, was one year older, a couple of inches taller, and a lot uglier. He wore a mustache and goatee and unlike his brother, he had had tattoos on every part of his body.

After learning that Leo had been arrested, Gerard made his way downtown to his bondsman to pay Leo's bail.

The two brothers ran the crack ring, but they never touched the stuff with their own hands. They had cousins and friends that they'd known from childhood who worked for them.

Leo always picked up the coke from their suppliers and dropped it off at different places. They had another cousin who was an expert at cooking the coke into crack. And then there were the street level dealers who sold it. The brothers collected the money from different houses and delivered beatings or worse to anyone who tried to fuck with the operation.

Gerard knew Leo wouldn't rat. He was their first cousin and the most trusted member of the gang. When they were kids, Leo always had their back in a brawl. And when the brothers stole a car and took it for a joy ride, and someone accused Leo, he took the rap and kept his mouth shut. He was too young for jail at the time, but it still proved his courage and loyalty. Gerard paid the bondsman and then he walked down just a few blocks to a nine-story beige building with metal grates covering all the windows, the Brooklyn House of Detention on Atlantic Avenue.

CHAPTER 13

Gianna had just fallen asleep when her brother barged into her room and dragged her out of bed. He forced her to eat a bowl of oatmeal and then he drove her to school and made sure she went inside the building and didn't come back out.

All day, she sat there in misery. Exhausted. Head pounding. Wishing for death.

She tried to listen to what the teacher said, but she couldn't comprehend anything. In regular school, she would have been in big trouble for looking like that, but in summer school, she was just one of many drugged up losers.

By the time school let out, she got a second wind. She snuck out of the building and tried to get out of there so she could call Juan Carlo, but Angelo was right there, waiting by the door. She was beginning to hate her own brother.

Angelo drove her home and then told his mother, "If she tries to leave . . . call Uncle Larry."

Gianna stormed up the stairs and into her bedroom slamming the door behind her and then she collapsed onto the bed.

CHAPTER 14

The sky was intermittently cloudy, but the hot sun was still in full force when Angelo left the house and met Pat and Mike at the Marlboro Projects, a complex of short and tall brick buildings with plenty of grass and common areas equipped with benches. People of all ages were out and the parking lots were full of cars. Two small playgrounds were packed with screaming children while an open fire hydrant sprayed cold water on bigger kids and young adults on a small street between the buildings.

When Angelo, Mike, and Pat entered the lobby of a sixteen-story building, they found a few young black men hanging around smoking weed. Angelo made sure that everyone there knew they were strapped, just in case. They spoke with some of the weed dealers who got their supply from Pat and Mike.

None of them had seen Gianna around there, and when they asked the crack dealers, they said they didn't know her either. They could have been lying, but for some reason, Angelo believed them. Gianna didn't have to go to the projects for coke or crack, it was everywhere by that time.

Pat and Mike drove away in their car. They had business to take care of.

Angelo parked his car near Frank's parents' brownstone in Bay Ridge then the two of them strolled to Big Mike's Gym on 4th Avenue, just a few blocks away.

When they went inside, there was a new girl working behind the counter. A beautiful young blonde with big hazel eyes and a charming smile.

As Angelo signed in, he glanced at her and said, "I haven't seen you here before."

"I usually only work here on Sundays. I'm filling in for the old man this month."

"So, he finally took that vacation."

Frank signed in after Angelo and said hello to the new girl.

Angelo introduced himself, "I'm Angelo."

"I'm Cara. Nice to meet you."

Angelo stepped to the side to take a protein drink from the refrigerator next to the counter. When he pulled out his wad of cash to pay for his drink, he got a good look at Cara's body. Round breasts that defied gravity, a tight stomach that showed her abdominals even through her tight tank top, and a juicy round ass that was so perfect, most black women would be jealous. His eyes followed her full hips down and admired a pair of legs that could have only been built through serious squats. Just looking at her spectacular body gave Angelo a hard-on, but he kept his cool and pretended not to notice her.

Frank asked, "You have a boyfriend?"

"No. No boyfriend. I'm just focusing on getting into college next year."

"Are you Irish?" Asked Frank.

She answered, "Half-Irish . . . half-Italian."

Two older women entered the gym.

Angelo and Frank got out of their way.

Frank said, "We'll see you on the way out, Cara."

She smiled, then turned her attention to the two women who had just walked in and wanted some information on gym memberships.

Angelo and Frank strutted through the gym wearing tank tops and shorts and showing off their thick veiny muscles.

Loud freestyle music played on the speakers above, barely masking the sound of iron weights clanging together.

They passed by a few skinny people running on treadmills, then a few fat housewives using cables and machines. Before arriving at the men's locker room in the back of the gym, Angelo and Frank glanced into the aerobics room to watch the women in tight pants get sweaty.

Angelo said, "A couple decent ones in there, but none of them compare to that new chick behind the counter."

Frank agreed, "I know. Fuck."

Angelo said, "If your dick was half the size of your beak, maybe you'd have a chance."

"Fuck you." Frank chuckled. "I didn't see her jumping on you."

"Give it time."

"Why? You planning to go for plastic surgery?"

They laughed while continuing to the back of the gym.

Inside the locker room, a giant bodybuilder with a head and face like a Neanderthal sat on the bench eating a pound of chicken salad from a Tupperware container. "What's up guys?" He was the size of Angelo and Frank combined.

Frank put a gym bag on the bench and opened it revealing small glass bottles of oil and flat boxes that contained pills. "I couldn't get any more of those 200mg Decas from Greece."

The bodybuilder replied, "Damn. I was looking forward to some more of those. And my costumers love them, too."

"I got some American Deca. Four ten CC bottles." Replied Frank.

"I'll take them all. Any more of those blue Dbols?"

"As many as you want." Replied Frank.

The bodybuilder finished his food, rinsed the container in the sink, then washed his hands. He opened his locker and removed a gym bag full of cash. "I could use some extra Winny . . . everyone wants to cut up for summer now . . . and some more syringes, too." He counted the money and then handed it to Frank, who then put it into his bag and then his locker.

The bodybuilder shook both their hands, then left the gym with his supply.

Big Mike, an ex-pro wrestler who owned the gym, allowed Angelo and Frank to sell steroids in his gym because they were his supplier too, and they gave him free stuff whenever he wanted to do a cycle. Angelo knew he could shake Big Mike down rather than pay him off, but he liked Big Mike, and they were all happy with the arrangement the way it was.

Angelo and Frank headed down to the basement where the free weights were located. It was mostly men in the basement, and it smelled like it. There were fancier gyms opening up here and there, but Angelo needed free weights, and a lot of them. Besides, no one doing jazzercise would be interested in buying anabolic steroids.

After some quick stretching, Angelo and Frank took turns on the bench press, first warming up with light weights, then pushing two plates for reps, inflating their chests. The steroids in their blood made their muscles and veins swell, as well as their egos. Angelo showed off by maxing out with three plates for one rep.

They spent about forty-five minutes in the basement doing chest and triceps with barbells, dumbbells, and dips, then they headed back upstairs where the air was a little fresher to finish up with some cable work.

Angelo noticed that when Cara changed the roll in the paper towel dispenser, she had to stand on her toes to reach it, and that added just a little extra bulge to her butt. He tried not to stare.

Scotty, a mentally challenged man, approached Cara and asked if she had seen any good movies lately.

He wasn't eavesdropping, but Angelo couldn't help hearing their conversation. He noticed how sweet and gentle Cara was when she spoke to Scotty. Angelo performed his set of cable flies while Frank flexed and admired himself in the mirror.

Two tall guys with a little bit of muscle and a lot of attitude approached the paper towel dispenser. One of them looked down at Scotty and Cara while banging his hand against his chest and talking with a fake lisp. "Uh . . . uh . . . uh . . . have you seen any good movies lately, Cara?"

The other one said, "You should have told me you like retards . . . I just happen to have a crooked retard dick."

Cara replied, "How crooked could it be? Your ex-boyfriend says you only got three inches."

"Yeah? You wanna find out?" He slapped Cara's ass.

It was so loud, everyone turned to look.

Angelo stepped away from the cable machine.

Frank exclaimed, "Oh shit."

The tall guy who just slapped Cara's ass said, "Very nice." He turned to his buddy and said, "You should feel this thing. Talk about buns of steel."

The other guy chuckled.

Angelo moved toward them. "Hey, Scotty. You okay over here?"

Scotty kept his head down but didn't speak.

Angelo scolded the tall guy, "How about I slap *your* ass?"

He stuck out his chest and protested, "You? Slap *my* ass?"

The other tall guy grabbed his friend by the arm and shook his head, warning him to stop. Either he knew Angelo's reputation, or he knew who Angelo's family was. Either way, he convinced his friend to back off with just a look.

The guy was much taller, but not nearly as muscular as Angelo was. None of that mattered anyway because Angelo was a like bull shark, half the size of a great white and twice as powerful. If he tore into him, he wouldn't stop, and the guy could end up seriously injured if not dead.

Angelo already had a reputation as a head buster, but he didn't want Cara to think of him in that way. So, instead of hitting him, he scolded the tall guy like a child, "Tell them both you're sorry and then don't ever look at them again. *Capisce?*"

The tall guy hesitated, but after looking to his friend once more, he turned to Cara and Scotty and said, "Sorry."

Cara nodded and then headed back to the counter.

The two tall guys continued their workout in another area.

Frank returned to finish his set of cable flies.

Angelo asked, "Scotty . . . you still have my beeper number?"

Scotty nodded, then stuttered, "I . . . I wasn't scared of those guys."

"I know you weren't scared. But there's nothing wrong with having friends that got your back. You need me . . . you call me. Got it?"

Scotty nodded.

"Your grandmother doing okay?"

"She's doing much better now." Replied Scotty, "My Dad keeps trying to keep her out of the kitchen. All she wants to do is cook."

"That's a good sign. It means she's tough."

Scotty chuckled.

One of Angelo's older cousins who lived in Bay Ridge had dated Scotty's uncle a few years ago, and even though they hadn't been together for a long time, Angelo always treated Scotty as if he were family. He patted him on the shoulder and said, "I'm gonna go talk to the new girl now. I'll see you later. Okay?"

Scotty nodded.

Angelo approached the counter and asked Cara, "You alright?"

"I am now." She answered, "Thank you."

He wrote two phone numbers on a piece of paper and handed them to her. "Anybody ever bother you again. You call me. The second number is my pager."

"Are you offering to be my guardian angel?"

Gazing into her mesmerizing eyes, it took all of his will power to keep from grabbing her and kissing her right there. He admitted, "I'm no angel."

Cara smiled, "That's okay. You're nice."

"Nice enough for you to join me at my uncle's Fourth of July barbeque on Thursday?"

"Maybe."

After Angelo and Frank finished their workout and left the gym, they burned a joint while strolling back to Frank's house. The THC in their blood instantly relaxed their twitching muscles. The sun was already gone, but the heat lingered.

Angelo approached his car parked on the street and opened the door.

Frank asked, "What's all those boxes in your car?"

"Fireworks."

"Nice. What do you got?"

"I have to drop them off to my uncle's friend."

"Oh . . . man."

"Don't worry, there's plenty more."

They shook hands then Angelo drove away.

His uncle's friend, Georgie Guff, also lived in Bay Ridge, that's why Angelo had loaded up the car before going to the gym. His trunk, back seat, and front seat were all full of boxes, but at least he didn't have to make two trips like he thought he would have to.

Angelo used the payphone on the corner to call George then they met in the parking lot down the block. They shook hands. George handed Angelo an envelope that he was to give to his uncle. They didn't speak about what it was, but Angelo already knew they were new credit cards stolen directly out of the post office, not yet reported.

After transferring the boxes of fireworks to a van, Angelo drove back home.

When he arrived, his mother was furious.

Gianna had snuck out of the house.

CHAPTER 15

This time, Gianna was prepared. She had taken her house keys with her before leaving.

Once again, she was worn out and ashamed after smoking crack and sucking cock. For just a moment, she considered suicide, but that was never her style.

With her dry mouth open wide and her eyes shifting uncontrollably, she slipped the key into the lock and turned it gently. The front door creaked a little when she opened it, which made her heart pound even more. Her hands were shaking as she closed and locked it.

Inside, she didn't go for the light switch. Instead, she crept forward in the dark relying on nothing more than her memory to guide her.

She didn't know what hit her . . . but it hurt . . . right across the face.

The lights came on. Angelo was in front of her.

He gave her another slap across the face and she fell to the floor crying.

He grabbed her by the shirt and pulled her up.

Gianna saw her mother at the top of the staircase watching everything. She wanted to cry out to her mother for help but she felt as if she'd already betrayed her.

Angelo dragged his sister out of the house and forced her into his car. When she tried to get back out, he met her defiance with a few more smacks.

Too tired to struggle, Gianna sat in Angelo's car, staring through the closed window at her mother who was now standing just inside the front door.

Angelo already had people asking around about his sister's friends and he learned that they were smoking crack and getting it from somewhere around Sunset Park.

He started the car and turned to Gianna. "You think I can't find things out? I know your little friends smoke crack . . . and I know where they go to get it." He started the car and headed down the block. "Now you're going to show me who you're getting it from."

Gianna hissed, "I'm not telling you shit."

"You *will* tell me. You think I'm gonna have a crackhead for a sister? And let you break our mother's heart every fucking day? I'll kill you first."

"Oh. Big tough guy."

"Shut the fuck up."

By the time they got to the end of 65th street, they turned right on 3rd Avenue, under the elevated rusted green steel Gowanus Expressway. Apartment buildings and houses lined both sides of the wide avenue and a strip of pavement in the center with parked cars and abandoned furniture, mattresses, and other garbage divided it.

As soon as they stopped at the first red light, crack dealers appeared out of dark corners and approached the cars and trucks.

Angelo called a couple of them over. "Yo. You know this girl?"

Gianna covered her face. Angelo pried her hands loose. By the time he turned back, the dealers had disappeared back into the shadows.

They continued forward, and then at the next red light, more dealers approached.

Angelo asked again, "Hey. Any of yous know this girl?"

Instead of covering her face, this time Gianna turned her face away.

The dealers moved away from the car.

The light turned green and Angelo moved forward.

A sliver of sunlight became visible on the horizon and Angelo knew the crackheads and dealers would be going back to their coffins for the day. He couldn't make a U-turn because there was a cop a few blocks away coming toward them from the other side so he turned left at the next opening, crossing the avenue, and then cruised down a side street.

There was an apartment building on the corner and then a row of garages on one side of the street and a row of decrepit old houses on the other side. Angelo noticed the cop passing on the avenue behind them. He didn't need to get pulled over for suspicion of buying crack. Especially with his sister in that condition.

He made another turn on 2nd Avenue and then came back up another one-way street with a few houses and small apartment buildings. "Don't think I'm giving up. We're coming back here tonight."

Gianna didn't answer. She just stared out the window.

Angelo felt like slapping the shit out of her again, but he had a feeling it would be for nothing.

Just as they approached 3rd Avenue once again, the light turned red. Angelo stopped.

Three guys came out of the woodwork. One of them said, "Hey Gina. Gina!"

"What are they saying? Gina?" Angelo asked, "Is that for you?"

"Oh my god." She covered her face once again.

"Gina." They got closer to the car. "What's up, babe? You wanna come party with us?"

"Party?" Angelo growled, "This is my sister."

One of the men spoke in a feminine voice, "Don't worry, big boy. You can party with us too."

Angelo put the car in reverse and double parked.

Gianna begged, "Please let's go. I promise I'll never touch that stuff again."

"You're fucking right you'll never touch that stuff again. But these wise guys need to know who the fuck they're dealing with. Stay in the car and keep your mouth shut." Angelo already had his Beretta in the back of his waistband, but he didn't want to kill anyone, he just wanted to teach them a lesson. He grabbed the Louisville Slugger from under his seat and got out.

The three guys from the corner were now joined by another guy they were calling Juan Carlo. He barked, "Hey, what's the problem here, man?"

"Problem? I'm just telling these little fucks not to sell to my sister again. And the same goes for you. You do what I tell you and there won't be a fuckin' problem. *Capisce?*"

Juan Carlo replied, "No one exactly . . . *sells* anything to her." He smirked. "And besides . . . it's a free country."

Angelo's mind was racing. What did that mean no one sells to her? Is his sister fucking these guys? For crack? His blood was boiling. His adrenaline pumping. As soon as one of them stepped within Angelo's reach, he swung the bat. The guy stepped back.

Juan Carlo came closer, hands in the air. "Yo. We don't want no problems here, man. Just go."

Angelo just kept thinking about these guys fucking his sister and giving her crack to smoke. He swung the bat and busted Juan Carlo's arm. Juan Carlo screamed. Angelo hit him again, this time in the head. He heard the skull crack as blood splattered all over his face.

Now standing outside of the car, Gianna was screaming for her brother to stop.

She had never seen him like that. His face and eyes looked like someone else. It reminded her of the exorcist movie, which made her sleep with the bible for weeks after watching it.

For a moment, she wondered if she were dreaming, but then she knew she wasn't dreaming when the unmistakable sound of a gunshot filled the air. It was so close her ears were ringing. And then another shot.

Gianna dropped to the ground and crawled along the sidewalk until she was safe behind Angelo's car.

The few people that were outside scattered.

She peeked around the car to see that her brother was not only still standing, but he was still pounding Juan Carlo's corpse with the baseball bat.

No one else was around.

She yelled again. "Angelo!"

He didn't stop.

The powerful combination of anger and steroids made Angelo resort to a primitive rage. He smashed and smashed as bones broke and blood sprayed. The wooden bat cracked, but even that didn't stop him.

The sound of Gianna's screams and the sirens in the distance finally broke the spell.

Once he realized that everyone else had scattered, Angelo raced to the car and jumped in. Gianna got in next to him and then he sped off, ignoring the red light, and turning under the expressway. He quickly changed lanes and merged with the traffic.

He wanted to get away from there as soon as possible, but getting pulled over for speeding with blood and brains all over his hands wouldn't have been smart, so he stayed below the speed limit and hoped for the best. His hands trembled from the leftover adrenaline in his blood so he tried to calm himself by smoking a cigarette.

Gianna said, "Oh my god. I think you got shot."

"What? I didn't get shot."

"Your head is bleeding."

He glanced in the rearview mirror and turned his head. There was blood, but no pain. "The bullet must have grazed me."

Instead of going home, Angelo followed 4th Avenue up and then pulled his car into the narrow driveway between Frank's house and his neighbor's.

Frank lived in the basement apartment of his parents' house. Angelo knocked lightly on the side door. He didn't want to ring the bell because he knew Frank's parents would hear it upstairs.

Frank must have been sleeping because he didn't answer.

Angelo knocked again. This time a little louder.

He heard someone coming up the wooden staircase inside so he whispered as loud as he could without speaking, "Frank. It's me. Open the door."

Frank opened the door and when he saw Angelo's head and Gianna's face, he asked, "What the fuck happened?"

Inside Frank's basement apartment, Angelo hurried to the bathroom.

Gianna surveyed the small living room and kitchenette combo. The old rug had lint on it and the small sink and countertop were full of dirty dishes and glasses. Big cans of protein powder and bottles of vitamins were stacked on a shelf above an old black and white television and the small fish tank in the corner had so much green algae on the glass that she couldn't tell if there were any fish in there. Everyone had always said single men were messy, but Gianna hadn't witnessed how messy until now.

Exhausted, she sat down in the small space on the sofa that wasn't covered with clothing.

The bathroom door was open and Gianna could see and hear everything that was happening.

Frank wiped the blood from Angelo's temple. "Yep. Looks like you got grazed. Lucky."

"So what should we do?"

"Just because I inject people in the ass with steroids . . . that don't make me a doctor. I don't know what the fuck to do."

The reality was now setting in for Gianna. Her brother was almost killed because of her crack habit. A tear dripped down her face, but she wiped it off and turned her gaze back to the open bathroom.

Angelo said, "Maybe you should stitch it up or something?"

"Stitch it up?" Replied Frank. "Who do I look like? Martha Stewart?"

Gianna said, "Martha Stewart writes cookbooks."

They all laughed.

She laughed even harder because of how they were laughing . . . but then she was overpowered by negative emotions. She broke down and sobbed. She hated herself and didn't understand why she kept going back to that stuff when she knew how fucked up it was.

Angelo came out of the bathroom and hugged her.

Gianna sniffled, then said, "You almost got killed because of me."

"Don't worry. I don't die so easy."

She giggled and sniffled.

Frank handed Gianna some tissues and then he handed Angelo a Band-Aid.

Angelo said, "A Band-Aid? Thank god you're *not* a doctor."

"And don't complain when you get the bill."

CHAPTER 16

Gerard was home in bed with his wife when he got the call about his brother Juan Carlo who was dead before the ambulance had gotten there. She asked what was going on, but he just told her to go back to sleep.

He left his apartment near the park and hurried down to the 3rd Avenue but didn't get too close because there were still police lines and cars with flashing sirens there.

The early morning traffic was backed up on the avenue as well as the expressway above, and the police activity only made it worse. The sun provided more and more heat as it ascended.

No one was talking to the cops, but Gerard's dealers told him that one of Leo's girls, an Italian girl named Gina, came with her big brother, and he was the one who beat Juan Carlo with a baseball bat. Gerard swore to god and his dead father that he would avenge his brother's death or he would die trying.

Instead of hanging around the crime scene, he went back home, got in his car, and drove up another fifteen blocks to his mother's apartment to tell her the news.

All he could do was hold her while she cried.

CHAPTER 17

After leaving Frank's house, Angelo wiped his fingerprints off the bloody baseball bat and then wrapped it in a black garbage bag before dumping it into a construction dumpster near Shore Road.

When they arrived at the Verrazano Bridge entrance, Angelo's heart raced as they waited behind a line of other cars at the tollbooth. The morning rush was in full swing. Luckily, most of the traffic was going into Brooklyn at that time.

With a handful of coins in the seat divider, Angelo was able to throw exact change into the basket and then go through without anyone even noticing him. They crossed the huge gray suspension bridge to Staten Island.

Even though the bat was gone, he was still worried about any blood that might be in the car. Or worse, he just hoped there were no witnesses who could, or would, identify him, his sister, or his car. He was counting on the fact that everyone there was either dealers or addicts and wouldn't talk to the cops.

When they finally arrived at Uncle Larry's white brick mansion on the south side of Staten Island, Angelo pulled into the long driveway lined with rows of flowers on both sides. He parked behind Uncle Larry's brand-new White Cadillac and stepped out of his car alone.

Uncle Larry was already outside, sitting on a wooden bench with a cup of coffee and a cigarette. At six feet tall and six feet wide, most people knew him by his nickname, Larry the Tank. He had the same face as Angelo, but older and harder.

Gianna stayed in the car. Angelo knew she was too ashamed to face their uncle, so he didn't push the issue. He approached Uncle Larry and told him everything that had happened. He left out the part about him suspecting Gianna of trading sex for crack.

Uncle Larry said, "I know how you feel, kid. But you can't kill every drug dealer in the world. As long as people want the stuff . . . someone's gonna supply it."

"So now what?"

"There's a good rehab right here in Staten Island."

"Let me take her." Replied Angelo. "I know she's ashamed to face you right now."

Uncle Larry told Angelo how to get there, and then Angelo got back into his Lincoln and pulled out of the driveway.

They drove past other mansions with manicured lawns and flower gardens and then finally turned onto a busier street that consisted of supermarkets, a movie theatre, and other stores.

Angelo and Gianna had been visiting their Uncle in Staten Island for at least ten years, so they had a good knowledge of most of the neighborhoods. It took about fifteen minutes to get to the rehabilitation center.

When they pulled up to the modern four-story white-concrete and tinted glass building, Angelo realized that Gianna would be missing the barbeque tomorrow if she checked into rehab. He considered letting it slide for one more day, but then he glanced over at her pathetic sleeping face and decided not to wait.

Inside, potted plants and flowers paved the way to the front desk. Despite all the foliage, the place smelled sterile, like a hospital. The waiting area was furnished with beige square chairs and pictures of serene landscapes. Angelo wondered if the rest of the facility looked that peaceful.

A smiling white-haired woman at the reception desk welcomed them and asked them to fill out some forms.

Angelo did the paperwork while his sister snoozed in the chair next to him.

He had never been known as the sensitive type, but his heart broke when an orderly in medical scrubs came to get his little sister and she began to cry.

The man took her through a door against the back wall and then, when they were out of sight, Angelo left the building.

He felt as if he'd betrayed his own sister. All the way home, he kept assuring himself that he had done the right thing and that rehab is what Gianna needed.

Once back in Brooklyn, Angelo pulled up in front of the house and mentally rehearsed what he was going to tell his mother.

CHAPTER 18

Agent Cortes had been in Manhattan court all morning, so it wasn't until lunchtime that he'd learned about the killing of Juan Carlo in Brooklyn. He didn't think it was the Ghost, because the Ghost was silent, and Juan Carlo was beaten to death by what the cops were referring to as a primitive beast.

Other than a body, a slug, and two bullet shells, the homicide detectives had no leads. Of course, no one in the streets would be talking to the cops.

Cortes wondered if there were any crackheads who had heard rumors and would be willing to sell what they'd heard.

He still had to spend the rest of the afternoon in court, so he called Agent Wicker who was at their office downtown and told him to go to Brooklyn to find out what he could. He hoped that Agent Wicker had learned something in their time together and could turn up some information that the cops didn't.

Agent Cortes planned on going to Brooklyn too, but it was late afternoon by the time he got out of court, and ever since his surgery, he got tired much quicker.

Cortes decided to call it a night. He was just too weak and tired to do anything.

He left the area of big limestone faced government buildings and hiked up to busy Chinatown where his car was parked in a multi-story garage. The sidewalks were packed and the sound of firecrackers and bottle rockets was everywhere.

The sun was still in the air and hot as hell. It had obviously rained recently because the sidewalks were still wet.

Sitting in his car, going west on Canal Street, he once again considered turning around and going to Brooklyn, but when his stomach began to cramp up again, he decided to keep going, all the way to New Jersey where his bed was waiting for him.

CHAPTER 19

He knew it would break her heart, but Angelo had no choice but to tell his mother that Gianna had been using drugs. He didn't tell her what type of drugs and he didn't tell her about his other suspicions.

Their mother was old fashioned, but she watched the news every day, so she knew what was going on. She cried when Angelo told her, but then she cooked him a big breakfast, and that made her feel a little better.

Angelo ate, took a couple puffs from a joint with his head out his bedroom window, then enjoyed a cigarette before falling asleep.

He slept on and off all afternoon, waking up repeatedly in a cold sweat to vivid violent dreams of him beating people to death and sometimes being chased and arrested by the police. That was the first time he had ever killed a man. He didn't feel any different overall, except for the dreams. He never expected to have such realistic dreams.

By the time he got out of bed, it was evening. The sound of thunder rumbled outside his window. The sun was still out, but it was pouring rain. He thought about Gianna and hoped she was doing okay, then he noticed a page from Frank, so he called.

Frank answered, "Yo. Where are you?"

Angelo said, "I don't know about going to the gym tonight. This weather sucks."

"That's alright. That new chick was more interested in me than you anyway."

"Hey. I already gave her my number."

"Well, you can't be that interested if a little rain will stop you from coming down here."

He knew Frank was just trying to get him to go to the gym so he didn't have to train alone. But it worked.

"Alright. Let me just eat something light then I'm on my way."

Downstairs, his mother sat alone at the empty table, obviously depressed.

Angelo kissed her on the cheek.

She said, "I don't feel like cooking. You want to order a pizza?"

"I'm good, Ma. I'll just eat a few egg whites. I don't want to get too full . . . I'm going to the gym." He knew she was going to play cards with her friends, otherwise he would have stayed home with her. "Everything's gonna be okay, Ma. She's only been on the stuff for a couple days. Now she's gonna get cleaned up and everything will be back to normal. It's not the end of the world. Trust me. I seen people get cleaned up before."

He kissed her cheek again and then opened the refrigerator. There was a bowl full of hard-boiled eggs. Angelo took a few out, peeled them, rinsed them, and threw away the yolks.

"I hate when you do that. It's such a waste of food."

"I told you . . . the yolks are all fat and cholesterol."

"At your age you gotta worry about cholesterol?"

Angelo was happy that his mother was arguing. That meant she was feeling a little better. He finished his egg whites and washed them down with a slug of milk then kissed his mother and left the house.

The sun outside was scorching and the humidity was suffocating. He pumped the air conditioner in his car all the way to Bay Ridge where he parked halfway between Frank's house and the gym.

When he and Frank arrived at the gym and signed in, Cara noticed the Band-Aid on his temple and asked, "What happened to your head?"

"I scraped my head at work."

"You must have a rough job."

"Demolition. Its hard work, but someone's gotta do it. So . . . what do you say about my uncle's barbeque tomorrow?"

She smiled. "Can I bring a friend?"

CHAPTER 20

Gianna woke up screaming. She'd been dreaming of Angelo beating Juan Carlo to death.

After getting up and getting ready, she was expected to help cook breakfast with the other rehab patients, but she'd never cooked before, so she helped with the dishes. The scrambled eggs were runny and the toast was burnt. She missed her mother's cooking.

Soon after breakfast, everyone sat in a group meeting where they discussed how pathetic they were and told stories of their drug and alcohol abuse. There was another girl her age with scabs on her face and a chip on her shoulder, as well as a boy her age with hair down to his shoulders, a sparse attempt at a beard, and bad breath that probably came from his crooked yellow teeth. Most of the patients were in their twenties and thirties. A fat loud black woman, a decrepit old white man, and a middle-aged man with long filthy hair and a beard who walked and talked like a zombie. Even the counselors looked like weirdos.

Gianna couldn't understand how that could help her. Looking at and listening to those losers made her want to fill her head with more drugs. She'd always just assumed drug rehab was about keeping people locked up so they didn't have access to drugs. She wasn't expecting this.

After the group meeting, everyone had household chores to do. She did what she was told, and prayed for the time to pass quickly.

Occasionally, she heard a stray firework outside and it reminded her of the party she'd be missing. But just when she felt her lowest, there was a pleasant surprise at lunchtime. A visit from her brother and uncle. Her mother wasn't there. Gianna knew how stubborn her mother was because she was exactly the same.

She kissed her brother and uncle when they arrived.

Although she'd been dreading this moment, she knew it would come eventually. "I'm sorry, Uncle Larry."

Uncle Larry hugged her and assured her, "There's nothing to be sorry about, kid. We all make mistakes sometimes. Just get better and get back home. Your mother misses you."

"Yeah? Then where is she now?"

Angelo objected, "Come on. Give it a rest already."

Uncle Larry said, "Would you want to see your only daughter locked in a place like this? Give her some time."

Angelo handed Gianna some containers of food, a box of pastries, and a carton of cigarettes. "You can share them with your friends if you want."

"These people are not my friends."

"Whatever."

Gianna turned her head to look out the window when she heard more firecrackers.

Uncle Larry said, "There will be more fireworks next year . . . and the year after that. You got your whole life in front of you. You're just gonna miss one party."

Uncle Larry made sense, but Gianna still wasn't happy about being there.

CHAPTER 21

After Angelo got back home from Staten Island, a quick but heavy downpour drenched the streets. The news forecasted pop up showers throughout the day. He hoped it wouldn't rain heavy enough or long enough to ruin the barbeque.

Inside, he took another quick shower and then threw on a pair of shorts and an undershirt. He looked in the mirror, and while he was happy about how big his chest and arms looked in the tight undershirt, he wondered if he shouldn't put on something a little more formal to look good for Cara. Then he thought about the heat and humidity outside, and how much he'd be sweating, so he decided to stay with the shorts and undershirt.

Outside, the afternoon sun was brutal. A couple raindrops fell, but it felt good in contrast to the thick humidity.

Angelo got in his car and cruised down 86th Street with the air conditioner on maximum, under the elevated train tracks while listing to freestyle music on the radio.

Traffic lightened up on 86th Street as the tracks above turned north and then eventually disappeared from sight. Angelo stayed on 86th Street, passing the Oriental Theater and then rows of small houses and stores as he made his way down the avenues. He turned at 14th Avenue, and then made another turn down a quiet residential street lined with two-family attached houses, each with a garage on the lower level.

Cara and her friend were standing on the wet stoop in front of Cara's house, leaning against the railing. A big American flag and a few 4th of July decorations adorned the small front lawn.

Angelo knew she was bringing her friend, but she didn't mention that her friend was Asian. He knew the guys at the barbeque would go crazy over her because of her cute little face. Cara's friend wore an oversized T-shirt that covered only one shoulder revealing a striped tank top underneath, and short jeans shorts as well as sneakers, but no matter how cute she dressed, she looked like a skinny child next to Cara.

Cara's straight blonde hair was crimped and her bangs were teased and sprayed up high in the front. Angelo tried not to stare at her deliciousness, but he couldn't help it. The white sundress with blue flowers that she wore wrapped tightly around her hips and ass and then contoured in to fit her tight little stomach just right. Her milky white breasts reflected the light of the sun creating a golden aura.

Angelo wondered if he was dreaming, but he knew he was awake when a sudden rush of blood engorged his penis. He adjusted himself then waited a moment before stepping out of the car.

CHAPTER 22

Every year since birth, Cara had gone to Pennsylvania with her parents and older brothers for the Fourth of July. Now that her brothers were both away in college and wouldn't be going, and because Cara's older cousin in Pennsylvania had become very creepy last year when he commented on how Cara was developing and then kept trying to give her unwarranted hugs, she convinced her parents to let her stay in Brooklyn for the holiday.

Cara and Wendy had been waiting in the house, but when the rain shower stopped, they went outside to wait on the stoop. She noticed that Angelo was there exactly five minutes early.

After locking her front door, Cara and her friend approached the curb.

Angelo stepped out of his double-parked black Lincoln wearing a white undershirt that showcased his muscular body as well as blue shorts with a white stripe down the sides and white socks up to the calf, each with a red and blue stripe at the top. His dark brown hair was slicked black and he was sporting a pair of Ray Ban aviator sunglasses. The sun reflected off the gold cross and chain hanging around his neck.

Cara whispered to her friend, "Isn't he hot?"

Angelo kissed Cara on the cheek and then hugged her. His big arms and shoulders felt good wrapped around her, but she couldn't stay like that all day, so she said, "This is Wendy."

Angelo and Wendy shook hands.

"So . . . I hope you girls are hungry. Because there's a lot of food."

"I'm starved." Replied Wendy.

Cara sat up front next to Angelo while her friend got in the back.

"I got you something." He gave her a tiny Teddy bear holding an American flag.

Pleasantly surprised, Cara touched with her face and said, "He's so cute. I think I'll name him Angelo Junior."

They drove up 86th Street, all the way to Spumoni gardens.

When Angelo pulled up at his uncle's block, Cara noticed Big Mike, the owner of the gym where she worked, double-parked in a brand new white convertible Cadillac Eldorado with the top down. A petite beautiful woman with short blonde hair wearing a leopard print bikini top sat next to Big Mike.

Angelo pulled up next to them and ignored the cars behind him beeping their horns. He rolled down the window and stuck his head out. "Yo, Mike."

Big Mike turned and exclaimed, "Just the man I was looking for! Where can I park this thing?"

"I wouldn't park in the street today with all these fireworks." Said Angelo. "Follow me. There's an indoor garage a couple blocks from here."

Big Mike followed Angelo up the street.

Cara said, "That girl with Big Mike looks so familiar."

"Yeah. She does look familiar." Added Wendy.

Angelo said, "That's because she's on a billboard in Times Square. Some magazines too. She's that new supermodel from England. They call her Lulu."

"Wow. She is beautiful." Remarked Cara.

It was only a few minutes before they parked in the garage and then the five of them strolled along Avenue U a couple blocks until reaching a street that was blocked with barricades.

Two small apartment buildings sat on the corner next to a pair of small garages. The rest of the block consisted of two-story semi-attached houses.

The sound of firecrackers was replaced by music from boom boxes playing disco, freestyle, and rock. Kids raced up and down the empty street playing stickball, hopscotch, and other games while old people relaxed on chairs and stoops and young adults mingled. Many houses had their own barbeques going.

Angelo said hello briefly as he passed crowds of people. Cara stood proudly at his side with her little friend next to her. Big Mike and his model girlfriend followed closely behind.

Cara knew Angelo was a rough guy, but she also admired him for his softer side, which she was reminded of when he went out of his way to approach a group of old women who were sitting on a stoop. He bent down and kissed each one them on the cheek, saying, "*Come va, signora?*" He said other things in Italian, which Cara didn't understand, but it turned her on to hear it.

Down the block, before the corner, was a parking lot, but instead of cars, it contained a huge barbeque and a few tables and chairs. A few old men played cards while others ate. Doo Wop music from the fifties played on a boom box.

Scotty was there eating a hot dog and quickly cleaned the mustard from his face when he saw Cara approaching. "Hi, Cara. I didn't know you would be here."

She responded, "Angelo invited me."

"Me too. They're gonna shoot big fireworks later."

Angelo patted Scotty on the shoulder, "I'm glad you could make it, Scotty."

Scotty asked Cara, "Have you seen any good movies lately?"

She replied, "Wendy and I just saw the Karate Kid last night."

"Oh . . . I love that movie. I saw it twice. Once with my mom and once with my dad."

Next to Scotty was Sal, a tall man in a black shirt who said, "What's it all about, huh? What kind of life?" He bit into a sausage and pepper hero.

Angry Jimmy, the man standing next to Sal, was shorter, ten years older, and had a mustache.

Angelo introduced them. "This is Sally Vegas and Angry Jimmy."

Joey, a small man with perfect hair, crooked teeth, and a face like a pug approached from across the street. "Hey, Jimmy . . . I heard you died last week. Did you see the light at the end of the tunnel?"

Angry Jimmy responded, "I saw darkness! Nothing but fucking darkness!"

Everyone laughed.

Joey then turned to Angelo and asked, "Why didn't you tell me you had celebrities coming?" He shook Big Mike and Lulu's hands, then he turned to Cara and Wendy. He whipped a comb out of his back pocket and began coming back his greasy hair. "And who are these *ragazze delicate?*"

Angelo replied, "Cara and Wendy . . . this is my cousin Joey."

Joey touched Wendy's hair and blurted out, "Oooooh. I like Chinese girls."

She moved away.

"What's a matter?" Asked Joey. "You got somethin' against Italians?"

Angelo pleaded, "Come on, Joe. You trying to scare the poor girl away already?"

Joey then turned to Sally Vegas and asked, "What's that, a new chain?"

Sal pulled the thick gold chain and crucifix out of his shirt. "Do you love it?" He showed it to Joey for a moment then he put it back under his shirt.

"You spend all that money just to hide it under your shirt? Why don't you leave it out?"

"That's how I like it." Replied Sal.

A man with shoulder-length hair and a mustache approached. "Tell me you got a fatty for big daddy."

Angelo was obviously trying to hide it from Cara when he slipped the man a joint.

Cara saw it but pretended not to.

Angelo introduced him, "This is Speedy."

After everyone finished shaking hands, Cara and the others followed Angelo to a man wearing an undershirt and almost as much jewelry as Mr. T sitting in a beach chair while two sexy women half his age catered to him.

Angelo introduced him. "This is Big Al. He's our resident playboy."

Big Al took off his sunglasses and warned, "You better hold on tight to those broads around me, buddy boy." He winked at the girls.

A balding man with a face and build similar to Angelo flipped burgers on the grill. Cara knew he must be Angelo's uncle.

The man kissed Angelo on both cheeks, then put his arm around his shoulder. "I'm glad your friends could make it. There's plenty of food. Steaks, burgers, dogs. These animals already devoured all the shrimps, but I sent some kids out to get more."

Everyone introduced themselves to Uncle Larry, and then they followed him to the cooler full of beers and sodas. The five of them sat at a table with plates full of food and cold drinks.

While eating, Cara whispered to Angelo, "Are you in the mafia?"

Angelo chuckled and said, "You're so cute."

CHAPTER 23

Gerard had never met Gianna but he'd heard about her from Leo, so he picked up Leo in his green Datsun 280Z and drove him to Gravesend so he could show him where she lived. He didn't know if her brother lived there with her, but it was the best place to start.

When they arrived, they found the street blocked off and a party going on.

They stayed in the car and watched.

Leo said, "Too many witnesses here."

"We don't have to get him today." Replied Gerard. "Which one is her house?"

"We can't see it from here. It's closer to the other end of the street."

Gerard drove up a couple of blocks, then made a couple of turns, coming back up the opposite way on another street until arriving at the other end of the block party.

Leo pointed and said, "That's the house . . . there . . . the red one on the other side of that parking lot."

He got a good look at the house but Gerard knew they'd have to come back another time and drive by it to get a feel of things.

"That old guy in the parking lot looks familiar." Leo said, "Wait a minute . . . oh shit . . . you know who these people are?"

Gerard heard Leo talking but his mind was on his revenge. "What are you saying now?"

"That old man over there is Philly Bones. And I recognize that other guy, too . . . he was on the news a few months ago . . . Georgie Guff. You know who these people are?"

CHAPTER 24

The DEA office was closed for the federal holiday.

Cortes would have rather been there working for free than to have the day off with nothing to do.

After spending a little time at the grocery store, Cortes managed to catch a short afternoon nap, but he spent most of the day after that sitting on his sofa going over his personal notes about the 3rd Avenue Ghosts while listening to and occasionally glancing up at baseball games on TV.

Even in New Jersey, there were firecrackers and bottle rockets going off everywhere.

Agent Cortes relaxed in the living room of his messy little house and ate a nuked frozen dinner while watching Jeopardy.

A couple of hours later, he tuned his TV to the big fireworks display.

He stared at the only picture he had left of his ex-wife and their dead son. His wife was a schoolteacher from Korea. He'd met her when he was stationed there with the army in 1960. He got her pregnant, but took responsibility right away and married her. Their son was born in Korea, but Cortes moved them both to America in 1963.

They lived in the suburbs of Los Angeles where Cortes worked in a warehouse by day and took college courses at night while his wife taught English to immigrants. Being busy all the time, he didn't have much time to spend with his family, so he never knew that his son had problems with other kids because he was of mixed race.

Finally, Cortes graduated college after seven years. At age thirty, he became a high school teacher and assistant football coach. By the time he found out that his son was using heroin, it was too late. His fifteen-year-old son died of a heroin overdose. Cortes applied for the DEA the next day. He had no prior law enforcement experience, but the combination of him being a veteran and the fact that drug abuse in America had recently skyrocketed out of control, Cortes was recruited by the DEA only a few months after he applied.

Heroin had become less popular when cheap powerful cocaine flooded the markets in the late seventies and early eighties. Cortes didn't care what drugs he was fighting, they were all the same to him.

One year later, his depressed wife divorced him and moved back to South Korea.

He poured himself a drink while watching the fireworks display on TV. As he sipped the drink, he wished for a cigarette, and if he weren't feeling so weak and tired, he probably would have gone out to buy a pack. Instead, he drank himself to sleep.

CHAPTER 25

The rehab had used air conditioners that were donated, so they didn't do much good. Gianna usually wasn't too hot, but it must have been brutal outside because inside she was sweating on her pillow.

She lied on the hard little bed and tried to sleep but between the sound of fireworks outside and the visions in her head of Angelo beating Juan Carlo to death, she stayed awake for hours.

Finally, Gianna broke down and prayed to god. She asked forgiveness for hurting her mother and brother and she asked for strength to fight her addiction. Even as she prayed, she craved more crack. No matter how bad it made her feel after . . . she still wanted the feeling of that first hit. She knew in her mind it was wrong, so she promised god that she'd shape up, then she finally found peaceful sleep.

CHAPTER 26

Gerard had planned on taking his wife and daughters to New Jersey to watch the fireworks, but instead, he stayed with his mother and told his wife to take the girls to her sister's house. At three and four years old, they were too young to understand death and it wasn't fair to take away a holiday that they had been looking forward to.

Both of Gerard's daughters resembled their gorgeous mother, and Gerard was grateful for that because he wasn't the most handsome guy around, and he knew it. His wife still wanted a boy, and so did he, but he wasn't as enthusiastic about it as she was because he already had a big son from his high school girlfriend who now lived in Puerto Rico.

He told his current wife about his son in Puerto Rico when they first began dating and it didn't bother her. Gerard sent money to support his son every month, but because his ex-girlfriend knew what his business was, she wouldn't let Gerard have anything to do with the kid. Of course, he could have taken her to court, but he was afraid she would open her big mouth about him selling drugs for a living.

His current wife, however, had grown up in a family of drug users and dealers. She had never known her father, but her mother's family were all involved with heroin, so that life was nothing new to her. And Gerard knew she would never betray him to the cops.

After kissing his wife and daughters, he drove to his mother's house and searched for over thirty minutes to find a parking spot far away from all the kids and their firecrackers.

Inside the newly furnished apartment that he paid for, Gerard's mother tried to feed him, but he had already eaten at home, so they sat in her living room with a cup of coffee, looking at photo albums of when Gerard and Juan Carlo were little boys. They lived in Puerto Rico then and life seemed so much simpler.

Gerard's mother was heavy and her feet were swollen from diabetes. She spoke with a thick Spanish accent. "We should have stayed in Puerto Rico. We never should have moved to New York." She sobbed again.

CHAPTER 27

Angelo had a hard time enjoying the party while knowing that his sister was locked in a room. He knew she would get the help she needed in rehab, but he still felt bad and he missed her. Thank god, Cara was there to help keep his mind off Gianna.

He put his arm around Cara while they watched the fireworks display put on by Uncle Larry's soldiers. All day long, they had been hearing firecrackers and M80's, and the kids had been messing with ground spinners, sparklers, and bottle rockets, but now it was time for the big stuff. They shot mortars from PVC tubes that exploded in the air and provided spectacular colorful displays.

Angelo glanced over to see his mother conversing with her friends, then he turned back to Cara and kissed her on the cheek. She smiled.

After the fireworks, some people began to leave.

Uncle Larry's soldiers recruited the neighborhood kids to help clean up the mess.

Angelo took the girls home. He dropped Wendy off first, then headed to Cara's house.

Sitting in the car, they could still hear stray firecrackers going off here and there.

Angelo kissed Cara, and she let him. Her lips were soft and moist. But when his hand went up to her breast, she stopped him. "You're probably not used to hearing this . . . but I'm a virgin. And I plan on staying that way until there's a ring on my finger."

He wasn't expecting anything. He didn't usually get laid on the first date anyway. But his testosterone was so high, and she was so beautiful, he had to give it a shot. But she said no . . . so he said, "I can respect that." There was silence for a moment, then he changed the subject. "I wanted to see the Karate Kid with Frank but he laughed at me. Was it really as good as people are saying?"

"I liked it. I don't know if you would like it. You probably would." Cara asked, "Hey. Why did your cousin ask that guy if he died?"

"Who died? Oh . . . Angry Jimmy? He did die. Two weeks ago of a heart attack . . . technically anyway. They say he was dead for a couple of minutes before they brought him back."

"Wow." Cara changed the subject again, "You know . . . you never did answer my question."

"What question was that?"

"Are you in the mafia?"

Angelo's family had come to America in the early 1900's from a town called *Castellammare del Golfo* in Sicily. His grandfather and his grandfather's brother-in-law both fought in the *Castellammarese* mafia war in Brooklyn and Manhattan and then fell into the Profaci family when the five families were formed in 1931. Angelo's father, uncle, and a few cousins were also made members of the family.

But of course, Angelo wasn't going to tell Cara any of that, instead, he told her what everyone in the family said when they were asked about the mafia, "There's no such thing as the mafia. Hollywood made that up to sell movies."

CHAPTER 28

Although it had taken her a while to fall asleep on the hard little bed, Gianna finally got some rest.

The next morning, she woke up feeling hopeful as she prayed to god once again.

She ate her burnt misshapen pancakes and half-raw bacon with a smile on her face, then she helped wash the pots and pans while humming a Duran Duran tune inside her head.

Later, during the group session, she finally opened up about her feelings and realized that there was something bothering her deep inside . . . and that was the loss of her father when she was only ten years old.

After lunch, the patients performed household chores then they had a little more free time to do whatever they wanted before their next group session.

Gianna spent her free time reading her bible and praying as she relaxed in the backyard. The bright sun and the smell of fully blossomed flowers made her feel warm and confident that life will be better.

CHAPTER 29

At the risk of sounding desperate, after dropping Cara off at home after the barbeque last night, Angelo had asked her to have lunch with him today. She said yes.

After another night waking up to vivid violent dreams, he finally got some sleep when the sun was coming out and then he woke up later than he had planned to.

He still had time before lunch, and even though he'd be working out at the gym later, he did a couple hundred push-ups and flexed in the mirror before his shower just to get pumped up before picking up Cara.

While passing Spumoni Gardens on the way to the barbeque yesterday, Cara had mentioned that she'd never had pizza from L&B before, and she was surprised to hear that the sauce was on top of the cheese.

It was hot and humid once again, but Angelo didn't want Cara to think that he only owned shorts and tank tops, so he threw on a pair of blue jeans, white Nike sneakers, and a Polo shirt. It was too hot to wear it, but he also took his brand new Member's Only jacket with him.

He picked up Cara and then drove back to Spumoni Gardens where they ordered a few slices and sat on one of the many benches inside a fenced-off area in front of the pizzeria and the restaurant next door. Cars and pedestrians passed by as people of all ages sat outdoors eating pizza and Italian ices.

Despite the brightness of the sun, Angelo removed his sunglasses so he could gaze into Cara's eyes as they spoke. "So . . . I noticed that every man in the gym is after you. Even a few women."

Cara belted out a healthy laugh that made Angelo smile.

She replied, "Those guys in the gym will go after anything. My father always told me how boys are . . . I always thought he was exaggerating until I started working at Big Mike's gym. You guys are even worse than my dad said."

"Hey. How did I get thrown in there with all those other guys?"

Cara giggled. "Okay. I'll give you some credit. You are much more polite and respectful than most of those other guys."

"Is that why you agreed to go to the barbeque with me yesterday."

"That's part of the reason."

Angelo knew he was no pretty boy, but he wouldn't have minded a subtle compliment to stroke his ego. "And . . . what else?"

"There was one thing I noticed about you that set you apart from all the other guys."

"And what's that?"

"You shave your armpits."

Angelo laughed. That wasn't remotely what he was expecting to hear. But he took it as a compliment anyway. "I can't be the only guy in the gym who shaves his armpits."

She giggled. "You're the only one I've seen so far. Those other guys are so nasty with their big bushes sticking out."

Angelo laughed loud, which made Cara laugh loud, then they both laughed uncontrollably while everyone around them turned to look.

After they finished their pizza, Angelo asked, "You feel like a spumoni?"

"I wanted to try one." Replied Cara. "But I'm too full."

Angelo had space, but he didn't want to eat one alone. "We'll get one another time."

They got into Angelo's car and spoke about what schools they went to while driving to Bay Ridge.

He double-parked in front of the gym then got out of the car.

The sidewalks were crowded with people shopping, women pushing carriages, and old men hanging out in groups speaking languages from all over the world.

Cara stepped onto the sidewalk and asked, "Are you gonna work out now?"

"Not with all this pizza in my belly. I'll go to Frank's for a while then we'll be back later."

"Okay. I better get in there. I start work in three minutes."

Angelo moved in to kiss her on the cheek, but to his surprise, she kissed him on the lips. Not a sloppy horny tongue kiss, but a quick peck. Still enough to catch him off guard and rev up the hormones in his system.

She hurried into the gym while Angelo stood there savoring what was left of the aroma of her freshly washed hair.

CHAPTER 30

Gerard had never been the emotional type, but now that his brother was dead, brutally beaten to death like an animal, he was filled with a lethal mixture of powerful emotions.

He was going to find and kill that girl's brother, but first, he had to bury his own brother and be there for his mother.

Friends and family were at the funeral home as well as hundreds of people from the neighborhood, some of whom he'd seen around, and others who he'd never seen before. So many people came that Gerard had to rent out an extra room and there were still so many people that some of them stood outside on 4th Avenue in the hot sun.

He noticed that the cops were there too, across the street from the funeral home in a gray van with tinted windows. When he had first seen them he felt like going over there, tearing the door off the hinges, and beating them to death just like that bastard did to his brother, but it was more important he be there for his mother. Revenge would come later.

Inside, everything was beige. The furniture and the carpeting were elegant but noticeably worn. Dim lighting and barely audible music provided a soothing atmosphere while the air conditioning kept everyone comfortable. There were so many flowers, Gerard hoped that his brother was looking down and could see how many flowers they brought him.

A big cross hung on the back wall behind the casket, which had to stay closed because the undertaker was unable to reconstruct Juan Carlos' battered skull. No one in the family other than Gerard had seen what had happened to his brother. He wished he didn't have to live with that image in his head for the rest of his life, but he was the one who had to identify the body and then prepare all the arrangements.

Gerard had spent most of the day sitting in the front pew with his mother, but he occasionally went outside into the heat and humidity for a smoke and to help his wife take care of their two little girls.

CHAPTER 31

Agent Cortes and Agent Wicker sat in their gray government van parked in front of a bodega on 4th Avenue, directly across the street from the funeral home. They took pictures through the tinted windows with a high-powered photo lens.

On their way there, Agent Wicker had said that he was uncomfortable staking out a funeral. Cortes told him that if things like that made him feel uncomfortable, he should consider another career.

They knew that the most experienced criminals spotted their van instantly, but there was no threat, so they stayed where they were, suffering in their sweaty box with the engine and air-conditioner off.

Most of the people outside the funeral home were there because they had gone outside to smoke. The cravings drove Cortes mad, especially when watching someone who knew how to savor a good cigarette.

A middle-aged Hispanic woman who looked twice her age with a full head of gray hair, on loan from the NYPD, was undercover in the funeral home and wearing a wire, but the two agents in the van lost her signal from the moment she'd arrived. It must have been wired poorly. Now they had no choice but wait until later to find out if she had gathered any useful intelligence, in the meantime, all they could do was hope that no one suspected the woman.

Lightning flashed and then a minute later, thunder crashed. A few raindrops fell but dried up instantly.

Everyone outside the funeral home hurried inside.

The lightning and thunder continued for a few minutes but there was no rain.

Agent Cortes noticed at the sweat dripping from his partner's forehead. "While they're all inside we might as well run the AC for a few minutes."

Agent Wicker started the engine and turned the air conditioner to maximum while waiting with his face in front of the vent for the cold air to come through. "I think it's safe to say they all know we're here. No point in sweating in here for nothing."

"You may be right. But if we keep burning gas, it will take a big chunk out of our budget. And as Nancy Reagan just says no . . . so does our supervisor when it comes to money."

More and more people came out of the funeral home and once again crowded up on the sidewalk as the rain lightened up and then stopped completely.

The undercover woman came out and asked an older man for a cigarette and a light, then she began conversing with him.

Agent Cortes hoped the intelligence they gathered was worth all of his suffering. The heat didn't bother him but watching people smoke was driving him mad.

CHAPTER 32

Angelo and Frank had returned to the gym that afternoon for a grueling workout and then Angelo went home for a shower and dinner.

The temperature finally dropped and the thunderstorms earlier had helped in bringing down the humidity. Before leaving the house, Angelo put on a blue FILA jogging suit with a plain white T-shirt underneath and kissed his mother.

He was going to pick up Mike, Pat, and Frank and then drive up to the Bronx to intimidate some bikers who owed Mike and Pat money for two pounds of weed. Mike wanted to drive, but Angelo insisted. He said it was because his car was bigger and had a better radio, but the real reason was because Mike's car was always a mess.

After all three of them were in the car, Angelo got on the expressway and headed downtown. They lit up a joint and passed it around. Angelo tuned the radio and stopped when he heard a Def Leppard song.

Mikey asked, "What the fuck is that?"

"Def Leppard." Responded Angelo.

Pat laughed. "What kind of band name is that? Why not blind cougar?"

"That's all he listens to now." Added Frank.

"It's good music." Declared Angelo. "What's the problem?"

Mike replied, "All those rock bands look like transvestites."

"I know. I hate that. I don't know why they gotta look like that . . . but I still like the music." The song came to the end and Angelo said, "It's over anyway."

Mike replied, "Thank God."

Angelo scanned the radio stations for something they all liked.

Frank exclaimed, "Hey. The Brooklyn Bridge."

Angelo responded. "Traffic is good here. We might as well stay on the BQE to Queens then take the Triborough."

The evening rush hour had already ended so traffic was smooth all the way there.

When they arrived in the Bronx, Pat had to give Angelo directions. They got off the highway then made a few turns through a residential neighborhood full of three-story row houses and housing projects before arriving at a dark industrial block with hookers sashaying up and down the sidewalks and pimps hiding in the shadows. At the end of the shady street was a strip club, an adult bookstore, a couple of auto shops that were closed for the day, and then the motorcycle club.

The club was basically just a bar that wasn't open to the public. There was one window but it was painted black and a row of Harley's sat parked out front. Angelo noticed that none of the hookers was hanging around on that end of the street.

Angelo parked his car next to the bikes in the hopes that no one would fuck with it. He then removed the Beretta from under the seat, clicked off the safety, and slipped it into his waistband behind his back.

The four eighteen-year-olds strutted into the club as the sun disappeared over the horizon.

1960's rock played on a pair of big speakers while men and women with dirty hair and beards and dressed in a lot of leather drank, talked, and laughed. Everyone stopped what they were doing and turned and gawked when the boys entered.

A tall bald man and a shorter man with long hair and a full beard approached.

The tall bald biker said, "We were expecting you earlier."

Pat replied, "We had other business to take care of."

"Come in the back where it's quiet."

They followed the two men through the smoky club.

Two older women with enormous tits served drinks behind the bar while a few people sniffed coke in the corner. The walls were adorned with old bras and traffic signs that had obviously been stolen from the street.

Angelo slipped his gun out when no one was looking and kept it down at his side as they entered a door into the backyard. They were easily outnumbered, and Angelo was sure he wasn't the only one there with a gun.

He could always come back with his uncle's entire crew, but then he'd have to explain what they were doing there in the first place, and he'd have to convince them that he had nothing to do with Pat and Mike's weed business.

Of course, weed was a much bigger money maker than steroids, but Angelo refused to get into it. He didn't want to take a chance of making any trouble for his uncle. Angelo's father had been killed six years earlier by the Maranzano family for moving into their territory with heroin. Angelo's uncle had always said there was nothing anyone could do about it because Angelo's father broke the rules by selling drugs.

While most young people didn't consider weed to be a drug, but he knew the old timers did, so while he enjoyed smoking weed, he stayed away from selling it. He didn't worry about selling steroids. Not only because they were not classified as a controlled substance, but because most people had no idea what they even were. And he could always use the excuse that they are hormones, not drugs, if his uncle ever caught on.

The small yard behind the motorcycle club was semi-dark and full of crates of empty beer and liquor bottles. When Angelo noticed that no one else was back there, he moved into a position where he could keep his eyes on the door, then, when no one was looking, he slipped the gun back into his waistband.

The tall bald biker asked, "Why the extra muscle? You don't trust us?"

Pat said, "It's not that."

Mike objected, "No. It is that. Every time we come here . . . you keep saying to come back tomorrow. We gave you the weed . . . we gave you plenty of time to come up with the money . . . you think we're some kind of fucking jerks or something?"

Angelo noticed the short bearded biker with his hand ready to reach for something. "Oh. Let's not get crazy now. Take it easy, Mikey." Angelo knew his friends didn't have guns on them, but he bluffed. "Listen . . . we could show you our guns to try and intimidate you . . . but we know you got guns too." Angelo noticed the short bearded biker second guessing what he was ready to reach for. "We could all kill each other right now . . . but then what? Will that solve anything?" Angelo whipped out a fat joint, lit it, and took a hit. While holding his breath, he mumbled, "Let's all smoke a little something, and then we'll talk like gentlemen." The first person he passed it to was the short bearded biker.

The short biker held the joint in his hand for a moment, then he smoked. By the time he exhaled, his hand was down at his side, relaxed.

They passed the joint around, and when it was finished, everyone seemed calmer.

Angelo asked, "Now . . . first of all . . . do you like the weed?"

"The weed is great. Everyone loves it." answered the tall bald biker. "The problem is the cash. I know it's not your problem, but we had to buy a new motor for our walk-in fridge . . . we tried to fix it so many times, but the beer kept coming out of the tap warm . . . we finally had to replace it. Then, one of our members got himself locked up and we had to post bond. Don't think we're tryin to stiff you. We got half the money right now."

Pat said, "That's a start."

Mike disagreed, "I don't know."

"I think they're good for it." Said Angelo. "How long before you can come up with the rest?"

"Give us a week. I'll take the ride to Brooklyn myself to drop it off to you. Everyone knows we pay our debts. And besides, you kids got the best weed this side of California. We have a prosperous future ahead." The tall bald biker waited for a response.

Angelo glanced at Mike and Pat.

Pat nodded.

Mike declared, "Okay. Next week then. You have my beeper number."

The tall bald biker turned to the short bearded one. "Get them their money."

The short bearded biker went back inside.

Angelo had his eye on the door, hoping the short biker returned with his friends' money rather than a group of bloodthirsty bikers. It was only a few minutes until he returned, and he had a paper bag full of cash.

They all shook hands then passed back through the smoky club to the street outside where Angelo was happy to find his car in the same condition that he'd left it.

Frank said, "I'm hungry."

Mike said, "You're always hungry."

Angelo said, "Let's get the fuck away from this place before we think about eating."

CHAPTER 33

The undercover woman at Juan Carlo's wake yesterday learned a lot of names and learned who was related and who was friends, but nothing more than that. Nothing useful about the gang and their drug dealing activities.

Agent Wicker was alone in the van, but this time he was parked a few blocks away and the audio signal from the undercover woman's wire was working perfectly.

Agent Cortes couldn't be there because he had a doctor's appointment.

He signed in at the doctor's office and waited in the busy waiting room for half an hour while wondering what was going on at the funeral.

A nurse finally called his name and then brought him into an examination room where she checked his blood pressure and temperature. Cortes hated going through all this nonsense every time. He already knew that after the nurse left, he'd have to wait a good fifteen minutes for the doctor, but he was pleasantly surprised when the doctor arrived in only about five minutes.

His mood quickly changed when he noticed the doctor's face. At that moment, he knew just what the doctor was going to say when he said it. "The cancer has spread."

Cortes asked, "How long do I have?"

"I don't give estimates like that. We're going to try radiation . . . and if that doesn't work . . . chemo. It's going to be rough, and there will be bad side effects."

He didn't have much to live for. If he died, no one would care. And his life wasn't so great that he wanted to hang on to it anyway. But there was one thing . . . the Ghost. If he died now, the Ghost would still be out there, helping to destroy America. He had to live long enough to take down his white whale. Then he could die in peace.

"Whatever it takes, doctor. I have unfinished business to take care of. I need to live a while longer."

"I like your fighting spirit."

The doctor's secretary made an appointment for the next day for Agent Cortes to begin his radiation therapy and then she gave him some pamphlets before he left.

Outside of the small medical complex in New Jersey, just as Agent Cortes was about to get into his beat-up little Ford, he saw a man at the corner gas station lighting a cigarette and then getting into his car and driving away.

Cortes left his car in the parking lot, walked down to the corner, bought a pack of Marlboro reds and asked for matches. On his way back to his car, he opened the pack and inhaled the familiar aroma of fresh tobacco. It made him feel almost nostalgic. He savored the smell for a moment then pulled one out, put it between his lips, and lit it.

He took a deep and powerful drag, then inhaled deeply. His nerves tingled with pleasure as blood rushed to his head. He enjoyed it for just a moment but then he began to cough. Harder and harder, so much that he had to hunch over while saliva dripped from his mouth. The cigarette dropped the ground, still burning.

When he was finally able to breathe somewhat normally again, he threw the pack onto the sidewalk and stepped on it, smashing it, and kicking it.

CHAPTER 34

Once again, Gerard sat with his mother all day at his brother's wake.

They sat there in silence, staring at the closed casket in front of them as people chattered in the background and Gerard's wife kept their daughters occupied.

When it was time for the evening break, Gerard and his mother didn't go anywhere. They stayed alone in the big empty room, still in silence. The funeral director didn't say anything. He just left them in peace.

Gerard's wife had returned fifteen minutes before the doors were officially open so she could give Gerard and his mother a sandwich. There was no food allowed, but Gerard knew the funeral director would look the other way.

His mother didn't want to eat, but Gerard's wife made sure she did.

Gerard didn't. He said he would eat his later.

Outside, he sat in his car, smoked a joint, and downed two airplane bottles of tequila. Glancing in the rearview mirror, he noticed the *Brujeria* store down the avenue. He'd never believed in magic, and he still didn't, but he had always been curious about the witchcraft that his mother had told him and his brother to stay away from since their childhood in Puerto Rico.

When the people arrived back at the funeral home, Gerard got out of his car and began greeting them.

CHAPTER 35

Cara wasn't sure how to dress for her date with Angelo, so she kept it simple with a black dress and black heels with her hair down. Of course, she sprayed on some of her new favorite perfume, Poison.

She wasn't ready for her parents to meet Angelo yet so she waited outside on the stoop for him to arrive. Her father was busy watching TV, but she knew her mother was watching from the window, she just hoped she wouldn't come outside and embarrass her.

Angelo pulled up, double-parked, and stepped out of his car.

He wasn't handsome in the conventional sense, but she was strongly attracted to him. Partly because of his masculinity, but also because of his confidence and good manners. Most men were either wimps, or went too far the opposite way that they were just jerks. Angelo was just right.

She liked the way he looked in his dark gray pinstriped suit, and without a tie, the thick strand of chest muscle that was visible under his open collar shirt made him look even hotter. He wore an expensive watch and he had a heavy gold chain under his shirt, but he never overdid it with the jewelry.

Angelo kissed her on the cheek and then opened his car door for her.

She appreciated his old-fashioned chivalry.

He took her to a restaurant that she'd heard of, but had never been to, Casa Rosa on Court Street in Downtown Brooklyn. "I thought about taking you to Manhattan, but I didn't want to gamble on a restaurant I don't know."

"This is fine. I've always heard good things about Casa Rosa."

Inside, dim lighting and white tablecloths provided a comfortable atmosphere and there was a fully stocked bar against the back wall. An older woman seated them at a small table in the corner.

Angelo ordered a bottle of Chianti, which Cara had never had before. She didn't know much about wine, but she knew red wine was supposed to be served at room temperature, yet the Chianti was served cold in a fat little bottle enclosed in a straw basket. She sipped it, and liked it, but didn't want to come home drunk, so she didn't drink more than a glass.

They started with stuffed mushrooms that tasted as good as the ones Cara's grandmother used to make, then they both ordered the chicken Parmigiana, which was served with Spaghetti on a big white plate garnished with parsley.

The food was so delicious Cara overstuffed herself. Something she didn't usually do. And although she only had one glass of wine, it went to her head.

By the time the meal was finished, they went outside where Angelo smoked a cigarette. She didn't like cigarettes, but she didn't complain. Both of her parents smoked, so she'd grown up with it.

After Angelo drove her back home, they stepped out of the car. He gave her a peck on the cheek, but she turned it into a long passionate kiss that caused her to get a little moist in the panties. She wanted him so bad, but she promised god and her parents that she'd wait until she was married before having sex.

CHAPTER 36

Angelo could still smell the perfume in his car as he drove to meet his friends at Pastel's. His dick was so hard that it hurt. He respected the fact that Cara was a virgin, and he didn't want to scare her away knowing she was the type of girl he could take home to meet his mother, but he had to fuck something before his balls exploded.

Inside the club, it was the same old crowd with only a few new faces. The dance floor and the bar were packed as usual.

Frank was out on the dance floor showing off his moves while Mike and Pat were chatting up a pair of girls who looked too young to be there.

Angelo noticed a chubby girl that had been after him for months. In the past, he had always been polite to her, but he didn't feel about her the way she obviously felt about him. But now, with his dick still hard and the excruciating pain in his balls, he took her down the block to his car and threw her a good hard fuck in the back seat.

She began by blowing him, but she used too much teeth, so he slipped on a condom, propped her up on the seat so just her fat ass was showing, and then pounded her from the back as she screamed.

He could hear people passing by and laughing, but he didn't care, he just kept slamming her until he was ready to blow. His mind was on Cara the entire time.

When he finished, he pulled off the sperm-filled condom, threw it out the window, and zipped up before she tried to cuddle with him.

He got out of the car and lit a cigarette. She asked him for one so he gave it to her. They stood there smoking while she kept going on about how good he had just made her orgasm.

Angelo felt guilty for the first time in his life. They weren't married or engaged, they weren't even boyfriend and girlfriend, but Angelo still felt as if he had just cheated on Cara.

After their cigarettes were finished, he said, "My friends are probably looking for me. I better get back inside. You coming?"

CHAPTER 37

The next morning, it was time for Gerard to say goodbye to his brother forever.

They started at the funeral home where a priest said a few prayers and a few encouraging words and then they followed the hearse to Our Lady of Perpetual Help, an enormous basilica made of solid white granite that had stood on the corner of 60th Street and 5th Avenue for almost eighty years.

Inside, marble columns held up decorative terra cotta archways.

Juan Carlo's coffin was brought up to the altar, under the statues of Jesus and Mary.

Incense filled the air while the priest's chanting echoed off the dome above.

After the church, they went to the cemetery where the priest spoke more useless words and then they lowered the coffin into an open grave.

Later, Gerard nibbled on his food at the restaurant. His stomach was hungry, but he just didn't feel like eating. He didn't even want to go there, but because he was the one paying for it all, he had no choice but to be there.

After dropping his mother off at home, Gerard headed back down 4th Avenue to the *Brujeria* store. Part of him felt like a fool, but the other part said he should get all the help he could get. He couldn't pray to God to help him hunt down and murder a man, so he'd try praying to someone else.

Still wearing his black suit from the burial, Gerard stopped before walking in. The sign above the door read, *Botanica*, and the front window was full of colorful jewelry as well as statues of Catholic saints.

Gerard opened the door and heard chimes as he entered.

Inside, shelves were full of spices, herbs, oils, incenses, and hundreds of candles with pictures of different saints on them.

An old lady sitting behind the counter, who had obviously been sleeping, stood when he came in. She spoke with a raspy voice and a heavy Spanish accent, "Can I help you?"

Gerard responded in Spanish, hoping it would make her feel more comfortable. "I just buried my brother today."

The woman also switched to Spanish when she spoke to him. "I'm so sorry to hear that. Are you here to make sure that his soul ascends to heaven?"

"Well . . . now that you mention it . . . yes . . . but, that's not really why I came here. See . . . my brother was murdered. Beaten to death with a baseball bat."

The woman said, "And you want to be sure the police catch his killer."

"Not exactly . . . I want to catch him myself."

"You have murder in your heart."

Gerard didn't answer. He just gazed into her eyes.

The woman switched back to speaking broken English. "I am sorry. You have come to the wrong place. Please go now."

The door behind the counter opened and an old man came out. He asked in Spanish, "That kid who was beaten with a baseball bat under the expressway? That was your brother?"

The woman hissed, "Mind your business."

"Shut up." Snapped the old man. Then he turned to Gerard and said, "I will help you."

The old man ignored the woman and came out from around the counter. He took two bottles of oil from the shelf and handed them to Gerard. "First, mix these together and rub a little all over your face. This will help you avoid detection."

"You old fool." The old woman raised her voice when she scolded Gerard, "You have no idea how dangerous this could be. I want nothing to do with it." She stormed out the front door. The chimes rang as she left.

The old man continued, "I can give you some prayers to wish sickness upon your enemy."

"That's not what I had in mind."

"I didn't think so."

As the old man burned incense, said chants, and waved dried animal parts in the air, Gerard's mind kept going back and forth between his skepticism and his desire to do anything that would help him find and kill the man who took his brother away from him.

CHAPTER 38

Agent Wicker and the undercover woman hadn't turned up any useful information the day before at Juan Carlo's wake, so today, Cortes had told Wicker to go to the cemetery in the van, but don't get to close.

The undercover woman was also at the burial, but Cortes didn't feel very hopeful. For a moment, his paranoia got the best of him and he wondered if maybe she wasn't already on the Ghosts' payroll.

Agent Cortes was planning to work half a day and then go to his radiation therapy in the afternoon, but when he woke up that morning, he didn't feel up to it, so he used a sick day, slept in a little longer, did his laundry at the local Laundromat, and then went to the same medical complex where his doctor's office was located.

As per the doctor's orders, Agent Cortes wore a loose-fitting T-shirt and jogging pants.

When he arrived, he signed in then waited.

Finally, an assistant directed him into a big gray room with a giant white machine that looked like something out of a science fiction movie.

A few people were there in medical scrubs with blue paper masks covering their noses and mouths. The whole scenario reminded Cortes of the surgery he'd just had two months earlier. The same fear he had then, now returned as they laid him down on the white table, and rolled him into the belly of the machine.

Blue light emanated from a circular window behind his head.

"Don't worry, it's painless. And it will be done before you know it." One of the technicians moved the giant mechanical arm to just above Corte's chest, turned the machine on, and then left the room.

The machine hummed for a few minutes, then the arm rotated around Agent Cortes' stubby body, and another mechanical arm was over him. The machine hummed for a few minutes again then the arms rotated again. There were four arms, and they continued to rotate around him and hum for the next ten minutes.

When it was over, the technicians returned and rolled the bed out of the machine.

Two of them helped him up. "How do you feel?"

Other than his usual stiff back, Cortes didn't feel any different than when he got there. "I feel fine. I could have done the whole fifteen minutes."

"Okay. But we wanted to be sure first. You have our emergency number in case of any complications later."

"I have it." Agent Cortes thanked them then said goodbye.

He felt fine when he got into his car so he planned on going to New York just to see what was going on. But when a sudden wave of extreme fatigue came over him, he decided to go home and rest. He could always catch up with Agent Wicker on the phone later.

CHAPTER 39

Angelo noticed the rain outside and hoped it would stop before he left the house. He put on his best black suit with a white shirt and a blue and black tie. His Italian black loafers were polished to a military shine and his hair was slicked back with a handful of gel.

His beeper went off. It was Frank.

Angelo called him. "I was trying to call you earlier. I'm not going to the club tonight."

"Why? What happened?"

"Nothing happened. I'm having dinner with Cara."

"You took her to dinner last night and she left you with blue balls."

"Her parents invited me. They want to meet me. I can't say no." He glanced out his bedroom window and was happy to see that the rain was gone. "Maybe I'll stop by after."

"Whatever."

"*Minchia*. What are you, jealous? I didn't think I was your type."

Frank laughed, then said, "Fuck you then. I'll just keep all the pussy for myself."

After hanging up with Frank, Angelo went downstairs and kissed his mother on his way out the door. He didn't have to worry that she'd be alone because some of her friends were coming over to say *novenas* for Gianna.

Outside, the humidity lingered. Angelo jumped into his car and turned on the air conditioner. It took a few minutes to cool him down as he drove toward Cara's neighborhood.

When he got there, he only had to spend a few minutes searching for a parking spot. He hurried to the house and on the way there, he hoped the house would also be air-conditioned.

Angelo introduced himself to Cara's parents.

The father was skinny with glasses and the mother was chubby with the same blonde hair Cara had.

He was pleasantly surprised to find window units pumping cool air into the living room and dining room. Their furniture may not have been as extravagant as the furniture at Angelo's house, but it was obviously of high quality and the house was well kept and had all the modern conveniences. The wood floors were polished to a high shine and there wasn't a speck of dust on anything.

In the dining room, they ate roast beef, baked potatoes, and mixed vegetables. Angelo complimented Cara's mother on the meal and took a second plate even though he was full, just not to insult her.

Cara's father was quiet most of the time and when he did speak, he had a timid voice. Angelo knew he was a highly successful doctor and an intelligent man despite the fact that he had a reserved personality. Cara's mother, however, was not shy. She asked Angelo about everything except his blood type.

He told them the official family story, that Uncle Larry owned a demolition and debris removal company that had been started by his grandfather. Angelo said he worked doing demolition rather than driving because he didn't have a commercial driver's license. He also said that his Uncle was preparing to give him a management position. Part of the story was true. Uncle Larry was a silent partner in the business, but none of them actually ever had to work.

Throughout dinner, coffee, and dessert, Angelo was on his best behavior.

Cara seemed quieter than usual.

After a couple of hours, Angelo shook everyone's hands, then left. He wanted to give Cara a kiss before leaving, but he didn't. He shook her hand too.

CHAPTER 40

After Angelo left her house, she could tell right away that her parents didn't like him. It wasn't just by the look on their faces, they came right out and said so.

Her mother said, "I don't like him. You don't match. You are extraordinarily beautiful . . . and the truth is . . . he's just not very handsome. You can have any man you want. Why him?"

"Because he's real . . . and he's good . . . and I like him."

Her father added, "He must come from a Mafia family . . . you know they always seem to be in the construction or sanitation business. In my day they were all . . . so-called longshoremen."

Cara had a feeling her father was right about the Mafia thing, but she didn't care. Angelo was a sweet strong man, and no matter what anyone thought, she liked him.

Her mother commanded, "I don't want you seeing him anymore."

Cara exclaimed, "I'm eighteen now. You can't tell me who to date."

"As long as you live under my roof I can."

Cara turned to her father.

He said, "I have to agree with your mother on this one."

Cara stormed to her bedroom and slammed the door. She slipped a cassette tape into her Walkman, put on the earphones, and turned the volume all the way up. The first song on her favorite mixed tape was *When Doves Cry* by Prince. She sang along with the words as her eyes filled with tears.

CHAPTER 41

The next day, Gerard found himself once again wearing a suit and sitting in church, under the eyes of Jesus, Mary, and all the saints. This time, they were there for Sunday Mass, and the church was full.

Sitting next to his mother, his wife, and his two children, Gerard recited the prayers but he didn't mean any of it. The priest spoke of forgiveness but all Gerard could think about was vengeance.

The only reason he was there, was because his mother wanted to be there.

After Mass, Gerard's mother stayed for the next mass, which was in Spanish. He usually would have come back for her, but he knew he'd be too busy, so he left her with money for car service.

Gerard dropping off his wife and kids at home then returned to the *Brujeria* store to buy more incantations from the old man. After that, he met up with his gun dealer and stocked up on guns and ammo. He feared no man. He'd kill every Mafioso who got in his way and he wouldn't rest until he avenged his brother's death.

CHAPTER 42

Sunday was his day off, and while it would have been the perfect day for radiation, the medical complex was closed.

Agent Cortes stayed home eating pizza and watching baseball games. A few times, he thought about cigarettes, but quickly remembered his last episode.

Memories of his childhood in Texas came back to him after watching a TV commercial about cowboys. Cortes had never known his mother or father. He was an orphan, and not a cute one. He lived in foster homes here and there, and unlike most of his counterparts, he never caused any trouble.

By the time he was in high school, the football coach realized his potential and put him on the first string. But when his foster mother contracted pneumonia and was too stubborn to see a doctor, she died and left Cortes without a home.

When the high school football coach learned about his situation, he applied to be a foster parent and took him in.

Cortes was well behaved. The coach and his wife, whose children had already grown up and moved out by that time, became his parents, and he loved them.

They had long since died, but when Cortes thought of family, those were the people he thought of.

He closed his eyes and took a much needed afternoon nap.

CHAPTER 43

Angelo was still having vivid dreams of beating Juan Carlo to death, but he finally stayed asleep, and somewhat peacefully. He felt well-rested after waking up.

By the time he got out of bed and opened his bedroom door, the smell of his mother's sauce hit him in the face. He wondered why she wasn't at Sunday mass, so he threw on a pair of shorts and an undershirt and went downstairs to the kitchen to find her in an apron hovering over the stove.

"You didn't go to church today?"

"No. Your uncle called me early. He said I should visit Gianna."

"I think he's right."

"I know. That's why I'm cooking."

"That's what all this food is for? What are you gonna feed the whole place?"

"Uncle Larry and his girlfriend, you and your sister—"

Angelo interrupted, "And you. That makes five. This is too much food."

"So she can give some to her friends."

Angelo hoped that his sister wasn't getting *too* friendly with anyone in there, but he kept that thought to himself. "Let me help you do something."

"Everything's under control in here. Just go get yourself ready. *Subito.*"

He went upstairs to shower and get dressed and was happy to see that his mother once again was being herself . . . feisty as ever.

With his head out the window, he took a couple puffs from a joint while listening to 1010 Wins, news radio. The weather report said it would be cool and cloudy all day, but no rain. Perfect for wearing a pair of khakis, a polo shirt, and his new Member's Only jacket. There wasn't any sun out, but Angelo brought his sunglasses with him anyway. He left his gun at home.

Downstairs in the kitchen, his mother was checking to see that the pasta was done boiling.

Angelo said, "Let me get that."

His mother tried to stop him from helping, but she couldn't.

He poured the hot water and pasta into a strainer in the sink. "What if they don't allow food there?"

She replied, "Your uncle already checked. He said we can bring food, but only on Sundays."

After his mother put the food into Tupperware containers, he carried them out to his car and put them in the trunk.

Then, when she was ready, they took the Belt Parkway to the Verrazano Bridge.

The wind was blowing hard as they crossed the bridge into Staten Island.

Once on the other side, they took another expressway a few exits and got off in a quiet residential neighborhood.

His mother said, "Staten Island is beautiful to look at . . . but who the hell would want to have to drive everywhere? Everything is so spread out."

Angelo almost made the wrong turn but then remembered just in time.

He parked in the lot next to the concrete and glass building that seemed out of place among the houses.

Inside, Uncle Larry was already waiting in the flower-laden lobby with his girlfriend.

They all hugged and kissed when they got there, then they signed in and entered the visiting area.

It reminded Angelo of when he was child and they had to visit his father in jail. It was a lot nicer than jail, but a similar layout with long rectangular tables and benches, and instead of guards, there were orderlies in medical scrubs.

CHAPTER 44

Gianna was beginning to feel positive about her future, and now that her family was there, she felt even better. The anger between her and her mother was suspended as they hugged and kissed.

As soon as her mother opened the containers, the smells of garlic and tomato sauce filled her nose and reminded her of home. The first thing she went for was a fried meatball. Crunchy on the outside, and cheesy and delicious on the inside.

She had met Uncle Larry's new girlfriend only once before, but she liked her. She may have not been as beautiful and sexy as some of his past girlfriends were, but she was much nicer, and down to Earth.

As they ate, they talked about what was going on in their lives.

Gianna noticed that everyone tried to avoid the subject of the barbeque that she'd missed. But it didn't bother her anymore. She was just grateful to have a loving family that cared about her, so she brought it up. "How was the party?"

Everyone was silent for a moment, then Uncle Larry said, "Same as always. You know. Barbeque. Fireworks. The usual. But next year, when you're there, I'm going to make sure we put on an even more spectacular fireworks show."

Gianna knew he was trying to comfort her, and she appreciated it.

Her mother said, "Did everyone forget about Angelo's new girlfriend already?"

"Ma. She's not my girlfriend. We only went out a couple times."

She pinched his cheek. "Sorry. I didn't mean to embarrass you."

Everyone laughed.

Gianna asked, "So . . . who is she? Is she wifey material?"

Uncle Larry said, "I'll say."

His girlfriend elbowed him playfully. "Hey."

"What?" Uncle Larry admitted, "She's gorgeous. You want me to lie?"

"You didn't think she was gorgeous?" Asked Gianna.

Uncle Larry's girlfriend responded, "I didn't get to see her."

"You didn't go to the party?"

"I was there early. But I had to work in the hospital that night so I missed the fireworks. I must have just missed Angelo and his girlfriend."

"We're just dating." Added Angelo.

Gianna said, "So . . . tell me all about her."

"What's to tell?"

"Where is she from? How old is she?"

"She's eighteen and just graduated. She lives in Dyker Heights with her parents. Her father is a doctor."

"Did she go to Lafayette?"

"No. Bishop Kearny."

"Oh. High class." Gianna had gone to Catholic school, too. From kindergarten up until the fifth grade. But, after her father died, money was tight, so she had to go to public school like Angelo. The only reason they even had a place to live and food to eat after their father died was because of Uncle Larry.

Gianna asked her brother, "What did you have to do to get her to go out with you?"

"I didn't have to do anything. No woman can resist my natural charm."

Everyone laughed, including Angelo.

Their mother said, "She seems like a good girl. I hope you stick with this one for a while."

Uncle Larry agreed, "Yeah. Don't let this one go, kid."

Larry's girlfriend playfully elbowed him again. Everyone laughed. He kissed her on the cheek. "You know I only have eyes for you, babe."

Gianna was happy for her uncle and her brother and all that happiness made her feel even more hopeful for the future.

Her mother asked, "Don't you want any *braciole*? It was your father's favorite."

It had only been six years since her father had died, but to a sixteen-year-old, it felt like a lifetime ago. She had been participating in the group sessions, but she got more out of her one on one time with her therapist there. She had learned that her drug use was just a futile attempt at filling the hole in her soul caused by the premature loss of her father. Gianna said, "I wish Daddy was still here."

Everyone became silent.

CHAPTER 45

After getting back to Brooklyn, Angelo's mother and her friends sat in the living room saying *novenas* for Gianna while Angelo headed upstairs to his bedroom where he stuck his head out the window to smoke a joint and hoped none of his mother's friends could smell it. He sprayed his room with air freshener and smoked a cigarette to confuse the aroma.

He had recently bought a hot VCR from some crackhead on the street but then had to buy the wires at Radio Shack to hook it up. Compared to buying a new one, he was still saving a lot of money.

After connecting the VCR to his bedroom TV, Angelo slipped in a bootleg copy of Trading Places.

He laughed throughout the entire movie except at the part where Jamie was topless. He pressed rewind and re-watched that part, twice.

When the movie ended, Angelo lay down on his bed and prayed to his dead father to look after Gianna and give her the strength to get off the crack and stay off it.

angelo fell asleep hopeful, and for the first time since killing Juan Carlo, his dreams were peaceful. Most of his dreams were about the pair of perky tits he'd just seen in the movie.

CHAPTER 46

When Gianna woke up the next morning, she was once again feeling happy and hopeful.

When she entered the kitchen, she asked if she could help with the cooking rather than washing dishes that day. They put her in charge of the scrambled eggs, which she burnt a little bit, but they were much better than the runny eggs they had eaten the day before.

As she and the others ate, Gianna noticed an orderly enter with a new boy. A tall and handsome new boy with thick brown hair, blue eyes, and a chiseled face.

She quickly straightened her back and worried that she hadn't washed her hair yet.

The new boy was obviously still a little high from the night before, and Gianna knew by his facial movements that he was on coke or crack.

The boy sat alone at another table and played with his food while ignoring all the others.

Gianna wanted to talk to him, but she decided to wait until after her shower.

When breakfast finished, she quickly got showered, blew her hair dry, then put on the best clothes she had there, a baggy white shirt with a blue skirt and cute little blue boots.

The new boy was not at the first group meeting. Gianna assumed he was in orientation as she was on her first day.

After group, they did their household chores, then it was time for lunch.

This time Gianna helped with the prep, cutting lettuce and tomatoes for the salad.

The new boy was there. He was noticeably cleaner and he was wearing different clothes, but he still looked like he was out of it as he ate his soup and sandwich.

Just as Gianna was about to approach the table where he was sitting, the director came in and asked the boy to come with her.

When Gianna sat down at an empty spot, she noticed some of the other girls whispering to each other and glancing in the boy's direction. Of course, there would be competition. He was hot. But Gianna knew she was by far the prettiest girl there.

After lunch, there was another group meeting, and once again, the new boy wasn't there. When they called her name and she wasn't paying attention, that's when she realized she was obsessing over the new boy and she needed to get her head back on track.

When it was her turn to speak, she passed. She had spoken about her father's death the past few group meetings but didn't want to go on about the same thing, and she really didn't have anything else to say.

As the others spoke, Gianna's mind once again returned to the new boy. She fantasized about how perfect their life could be together. They would both get cleaned up, graduate high school, have a big wedding, buy a house in New Jersey, and have two boys and a girl. She even thought about the names she'd give to her imagined children.

After group, they had free time.

When Gianna still didn't see the new boy around, she went back to her room where she read the bible and prayed to god to continue giving her the strength she needed to resist using drugs. And although she knew she shouldn't, she asked god to let the new boy like her.

CHAPTER 47

Agent Cortes had no choice but to take another sick day because there were no available afternoon appointments for his radiation therapy, and if he was going to feel as worn out as he had on Saturday, he knew he'd need time to rest.

He wondered how much progress he was losing by not being out on the streets. He trusted Agent Wicker with his life, but he knew he was a stickler for rules and regulations. He had given the young agent that as a nickname, *Wicker the Stickler.* Of course, after seeing the expression on the young agent's face in response to that nickname, he never said it again.

This time, the waiting room at the cancer center was packed and Agent Cortes had to wait for almost an hour. Of course, they apologized, and he knew he wasn't going anywhere afterword anyway, but he still didn't like being made to wait.

Back in the room and inside the radiation machine, he went for the entire fifteen minutes. It was the same as last time. He felt fine until about twenty minutes later, then he felt exhausted.

For just a moment, he considered giving up again. Early retirement or disability. They'd probably give it to him without question knowing he'd be dead soon anyway. But there was one thing keeping him alive. His stubbornness. He had to finish what he started. He had to catch the Ghost or die trying.

CHAPTER 48

Before dinner, Gianna had a one-on-one session with her therapist who once again asked about the death of her father and about the memories she had of him while she was growing up. The therapist also asked how things were going with her mother and Gianna was happy to report that they were talking again.

For the first time, they asked Gianna to prepare the main course, shake and bake chicken. The instructions were clear. All she had to do was place the chicken parts in the bag and shake them around. She'd never seen her mother doing anything like that, but it seemed easy enough.

Just as she placed the seasoned chicken pieces into a pan, she noticed the new boy coming into the kitchen.

The director asked the new boy to wash dishes. The boy had a bad attitude and refused to help, but his defiance only made Gianna more attracted to him.

During dinner, she managed to get a seat next to him. As he bit into his chicken, Gianna asked, "How's the chicken?"

"I hate shake and bake."

Once again, that bad boy attitude involuntarily turned her on. "I'm Gianna."

"What's up? I'm Kevin." It wasn't a full smile, just a little bit on the side of his mouth, but it was enough to make her tingle on the inside.

A loud obnoxious blonde girl with teeth like a horse stood and leaned forward with her hand out. "Hi, Kevin. I'm Michelle."

Not only was he smiling, but Kevin's eyes were sparkling when he gazed at her and shook her hand.

Gianna couldn't understand why Kevin would be so happy to make the acquaintance of this long-faced ugly bitch until she noticed what his eyes were focused on. As she was bent forward, Michelle's enormous tits were busting out of her already low neckline. And she knew what she was doing because she stayed like that until one of the orderlies told her to sit back down.

The big-titted blonde whore still had Kevin's attention as she ate. While gazing into his eyes, she placed every bite into her mouth as if it was a caramel covered cock. Kevin couldn't keep his eyes off her.

Gianna had A-cups and she barely weighed 105 pounds with her clothes on, but she was so much more beautiful than horse face Michelle. It was so unfair. Kevin was supposed to be her soul mate.

She kept her cool through dinner and then as they cleaned up, but when she went back to her room, she didn't read her bible or pray, instead, she put her face in her pillow and cried.

CHAPTER 49

Cara was working behind the counter at the gym. Her eyes lit up when Angelo came in with Frank. "Hey, guys." She wanted to give Angelo a big hug and a kiss. She knew Big Mike wouldn't have minded, but she didn't want the other guys at the gym getting ideas, so she kept it professional.

Angelo and Frank signed in, then they both shook hands with Big Mike who was sitting at the table in the corner doing some kind of paperwork.

Ten-year-old rock music played on the speakers above while Angelo and Frank approached the dumbbells.

A woman approached the front desk and said, "The paper towels just ran out."

Cara knew that if Big Mike had seen the unnecessarily huge wad of paper already in the woman's hand that he'd say something, so Cara didn't say anything that might make him look up. She just came out from around the counter, took a new roll of paper from the closet, and then proceeded to the towel dispenser.

She noticed the two tall disrespectful guys nearby and hoped they didn't say anything this time as she stood on her toes to reach the dispenser.

The two tall guys were there with two other guys who were not as tall but just as obnoxious. When they had entered and signed in earlier, Big Mike was behind the counter with Cara, so they were on their best behavior.

The same one that bothered her last time spoke again, this time to the other guys, "See. What'd I tell you? Buns of steel."

Cara ignored him.

He approached her and said, "Listen, honey. I know we got off to a bad start . . . let's be friends."

She knew he was just being a jerk but she didn't want to start any trouble, especially knowing Angelo was there, so she agreed, "Fine. Friends."

As she tried to slip by him, he stepped in front of her. "So . . . how about a drink later. Just as friends, of course."

The other three guys were laughing in the background.

"I don't drink." As she tried to maneuver around him, he refused to let her pass.

Cara didn't see where he came from, but Angelo was right there, next to the tall guy who was blocking her way. She noticed the tall guy's three friends approaching as well as Frank and she was afraid of what could happen next.

She glanced over at Big Mike in the far corner still doing his paperwork at the table, not noticing what was going on.

Angelo boomed, "Oh! What did I tell you?"

The tall guy turned to Angelo. "You really think who the fuck you are. Don't you?"

With an open hand, Angelo bitch slapped the tall guy, right across the face with so much power that the tall guy stumbled backward and then fell to the floor with a thump.

Some of the people gasped as the tall guy went down, others chuckled, but most of them just got out of the way.

Cara stepped back, unsure of what to do.

The guy's three friends jumped on Angelo. Frank jumped on them. Everyone was swinging wild punches, but mostly wrestling.

Everything happened fast, but it seemed to Cara as if things were happening in slow motion.

Big Mike was on his way over. "Hey! No fighting in my gym!" He grabbed one of the guys that was on Frank and then lost his balance and fell.

Now they were all on the ground, wrestling, and trying to get in a good shot on each other.

Cara didn't know what happened at first but there was a lot of blood.

The tall guy who had started the trouble shrieked when Angelo slammed his face with a twenty-five-pound plate. The plate fell to the floor. Angelo used his fists. The tall guy lifted his hands to protect his face, but Angelo kept swinging with pure rage in his eyes.

The tall guy dropped his hands. With his fists, Angelo battered the tall guy's face while everyone else was still wrestling and taking wild shots at each other.

When Cara noticed teeth in a puddle of blood on the rubber floor, her stomach became queasy.

She was happy when Angelo came to her rescue, and she even felt proud when he slapped that obnoxious tall jerk across the face, but to pummel a man almost to death, with such rage, she knew she couldn't spend the rest of her life with such a violent man. Her eyes filled with tears.

CHAPTER 50

Gerard picked up his mother and brought her to his apartment while his wife cooked a *paella*.

When he arrived back home, he helped his mother up the stairs to the second floor.

He could smell the aroma of the seafood before opening the door.

Inside, Leo was there, on the sofa with a beer in his hand while Gerard's daughters played with dolls on the carpeted floor. Leo stood to hug and kiss his aunt.

Gerard said, "Come over here and give your grandma a kiss."

The little girls got up to hug and kiss their grandmother.

The spacious two-bedroom corner apartment was furnished with basic but new furniture. There was a TV in every room and concert size speakers in the living room along with a high-end Sony stereo system that included a compact disc player. Gerard's wife wore the best clothes and his kids played with the best toys.

Everyone ate in the kitchen, then after dinner, the girls went back to playing in the living room. Gerard's mother stayed in her seat at the kitchen table while Gerard's wife washed the dishes, and Gerard and Leo went outside.

They strolled along the edge of Sunset Park.

Leo said, "I can't find Gina nowhere. She's not answering her beeper and none of her friends has seen her. I did find out about her brother. His name is Angelo. And they live in the same house. It's just them and their mother. Rumor has it that their uncle is a big time Mafia guy."

"And what about the brother?" Asked Gerard.

"He just graduated from Lafayette high school a couple weeks ago."

"He's a kid?"

"He's eighteen and was a linebacker on the football team. He may be a kid, but he's a big fucking kid."

"My forty-five don't care how big he is."

Leo chuckled.

Gerard said, "I wish I could do it myself. But those fucking cops would know it's me right away. Go talk to Cheo and tell him I'm going to double his regular fee. I'll be in court Thursday morning. Tell him to do it then. That gives him two full days to follow him and prepare. Thursday morning . . . 9 AM."

CHAPTER 51

After dinner, instead of watching TV in the common area with the other patients, Gianna went to her room to read her bible once again, but she couldn't concentrate. All she could think about was the new boy and realized that her hopes and dreams had just been foolish and childish.

She then wondered if her whole rehabilitation wasn't also just a childish fantasy. Did she really have the strength to say no after going back outside? She couldn't even say no in her dreams.

Depression and negative thoughts filled her mind for the next hour and then something came over her. The same feeling of defiance she'd had before she got there.

She got dressed, snuck down the hall, and then crept down the stairs to the first floor where she entered the laundry and storage rooms. There was a back door that the deliverymen used, and it was locked from the inside.

Gianna opened the door and walked right out of the building.

CHAPTER 52

After the fight at the gym, Big Mike told Angelo and Frank to get out of there before the cops arrived, and that he would cover for them.

Angelo went home and took a shower to wash off all the blood, then sat on his bed and thought about what he'd done. He had a feeling Cara would never speak to him again. He knew he had gone too far.

Later that night, he decided to call Cara and explain that he was on steroids and that's what had made him so aggressive. He knew it wasn't a good enough excuse, but it was the only one he had. And he couldn't stand to lose her. He called her at home, and to his surprise, she answered.

"I'm so sorry about what happened."

Cara admitted, "My parents didn't want me going out with you in the first place. Now I'm sorry to have to say . . . they were right. I can't see you anymore."

"You never told me they said that. I thought they liked me."

"They say you're a gangster. My father knew it right away. And don't try to tell me there's no such thing as a mafia. I may not be a world traveler . . . but I watch the news once in a while. And I know what's going on . . . I'm not an idiot."

Angelo noticed that his Uncle had paged him three times in the past few minutes and he wondered what could be so urgent. He wanted to stay on the phone with Cara and beg her to give him another chance, but he decided to give her some time. "Don't write me off so fast. Please . . . just think about forgiving me. I'll wait for you to call me. If you don't call . . . then I'll understand . . . but I'll wait, and I hope you can forgive me."

She didn't respond either way, she just said, "Goodbye Angelo." And then hung up the phone.

Angelo wondered if she meant goodbye forever, and while his heart filled with emotions, his beeper went off again. He quickly regained his composure, then called his uncle.

Uncle Larry said, "I've been trying to call you but the line was busy. I paged you four times."

"Sorry Uncle Larry, I was on the phone and I didn't check my beeper until just now."

"Your sister went AWOL. They say she slipped out the service entrance after dinner. You know where she might go?"

"I have an idea." Angelo got his Beretta and the entire box of bullets as well as a switchblade and a new baseball bat.

CHAPTER 53

After making her way through the quiet residential neighborhood, Gianna finally ended up on the main avenue just to find that most of the stores had already closed.

She would have taken the bus back to Brooklyn, but she didn't even have the little bit of change she needed for that, and besides, the bus was agonizingly slow.

A neon sign that read, *car service,* was visible from a block away. With no money, she couldn't go in there and ask the dispatcher for a car, so she approached one of the drivers who was sitting in his car, sipping on a cup of coffee.

She knocked on the driver's window.

A middle-aged, middle-eastern man rolled it down and asked, "Can I help you?"

"I need a ride to Brooklyn."

"Did you go inside?"

"No."

"I must get a price." He glanced over at the open store and picked up his radio.

"Wait." Gianna stopped him from making the call. "You can't ask for a price. I don't have any money."

"Well, I can't take you for free."

She was in no way attracted to the man, but she needed a ride, and she had sucked so many dicks in the past few months, what was one more? She said, "I'll suck your dick."

"Excuse me?"

She reached into the car and grabbed his penis through his slacks. She squeezed it lightly and felt it respond. "I'll suck your dick for a ride to Brooklyn."

The man was speechless as he looked around the desolate area and then back down at Gianna's hand on his crotch. He scanned the area, then whispered, "Get in. Hurry up."

Gianna went around to the passenger side and got into the car. The man drove away. Gianna noticed the dispatcher coming out onto the sidewalk and waving in the direction of the car.

A minute later, a man's voice said something in Arabic over the radio. The driver responded, also in Arabic. They went back and forth while Gianna massaged the man's penis through his pants, getting it ready.

When he finished on the radio, Gianna unzipped him and went down. She took her time, not because she wanted to savor it, but she was worried that if he blew his load too fast then he might change his mind about driving all the way to Brooklyn and throw her out of the car somewhere in the middle of Staten Island.

A couple of times, she felt him twitch, so she stopped for a moment and whispered in his ear, "Not so fast."

She glanced up when she noticed bright lights. They were approaching the Verrazano Bridge.

Once they were on the bridge, and Gianna knew he couldn't turn back, she finished him off then spit his cum out the window.

The man was obviously satisfied, because when he finally dropped her off on 6th avenue and 60th Street, he handed her a twenty-dollar bill and said, "A beautiful young girl shouldn't be walking around with no money in her pocket."

She proceeded a few blocks to the payphone outside Leo's building and paged him. She was worried that he wouldn't answer her page, but he did, and within a few minutes.

He told her to meet him at his friend's apartment just a few blocks away.

When she arrived at the building, Leo told her to be quiet as they went down a dark set of stairs to a musty concrete basement full of junk.

She realized that all that praying and all those positive thoughts were wasted now. She was right back where she started. She felt disgusted with herself and was ready to walk out of there and call the rehab, but she changed her mind when Leo loaded a fresh rock into a new stem and put it to her mouth.

Gianna slowly warmed up the glass as the rock bubbled. She inhaled. There it was—the first hit—helicopters in her head lifted her mind into the clouds.

Once again, as the feeling began to subside, the only thing that mattered was getting another hit, and another hit.

CHAPTER 54

Angelo picked up Frank in Bay Ridge then drove down 3rd Avenue until they were under the Gowanus Expressway. Instead of just going to random blocks, he drove to the same street where he'd beaten Juan Carlo to death. There were at least two other people there who knew his sister.

He remembered them calling her Gina, so when he pulled up and the dealers approached, he asked, "Anyone here know a girl named Gina?"

They didn't answer him. They just got away from the car when they realized they weren't there to buy anything.

Angelo knew that he and Frank probably looked like cops, especially since they were obviously not strung out. But he felt better with Frank there. Not just to watch his back, but to stop him before he beat someone else to death.

They rolled up to the corner and spotted a few other dealers. Still, Angelo didn't recognize any of them. This time he had some money in his hand so they could see it as they approached. "You know a girl named Gina? A skinny little Italian girl with long black hair?"

One of them answered, "I know who you're talking about. I haven't seen her in a couple a weeks."

A fat guy with a backward Mets cap said, "I got girls. No Italian girls, but I got some hot Spanish chicks. Just around the corner." He glanced over at Frank. "I'll give you a special if you take two."

Angelo answered. "I'm only interested in Gina."

They moved away from his car then Angelo drove to the corner and made the turn.

He turned down the next block and saw the guy who had shot at him the night he and Gianna were there.

When the guy saw Angelo's car, he bolted.

Angelo skidded down the street after him and then jumped out of his car and chased the guy around the corner.

Dealers and addicts scattered.

The guy was small and limber and climbed over a fence before Angelo could get to him. Lights were coming on in people's houses and apartments and dogs were barking as Angelo grabbed the flimsy fence and realized there was no way he was going to get over it and get to that little bastard in time, especially now that he could hear sirens in the distance getting closer. He was also worried about his car being recognized from the other night, so he gave up his pursuit and hurried back around the corner.

Frank was in the driver's seat of Angelo's Lincoln. He backed up down the street and then waited for Angelo to jump in before taking off.

Angelo tried to catch his breath. "That little fuck was there that night. He's the one that was calling her Gina. He's the one who shot at me."

"We should let things cool down for now, then come back with another car. As soon as they saw you they made a run for it."

Angelo replied, "I know someone who can get me a car. But what am I gonna tell my mother now after coming home without Gianna?"

CHAPTER 55

Leo called Gerard to tell him that Gianna just happened to show up on his doorstep.

Gerard told his wife to go back to sleep then he put on a pair of black jeans, black boots, and a black sweatshirt with the hood pulled up over his head. Staying out of the light just in case anyone in his building was peeking out their window, he hurried on foot to where Leo had Gianna.

It wasn't part of the plan, but when he got there and saw how pretty she was, he decided to fuck her before interrogating her about her brother.

Leo introduced Gerard and Gianna, but Gianna was so high she could barely speak. Leo handed her a big rock and Gerard watched her bulging eyes bulge even more. She broke off a big chunk, put it in the pipe, and smoked it.

Gerard asked Leo for a condom then he made Gianna lie back on a small dusty table. He stood in front of her and slipped it in, but the motions she made with her mouth were too distracting, so he took it out, pulled her up, and bent her over. The condom was pre-lubricated so he slipped it right into her ass. She tried to resist, but Leo helped hold her down. Gerard pounded her ass until he was finished, then he smoked a cigarette while watching the pathetic little girl take another hit from the pipe while her pants were still down around her ankles.

He considered the fact that killing her brother wouldn't punish him for what he had done to Juan Carlo. For him to suffer, he'd have to experience the same loss that Gerard had experienced. To make Angelo suffer, Gerard knew he had to kill Gianna. And as a bonus, he wouldn't have to pay Cheo to find and kill her Angelo.

Instead of killing her in a conventional manner and then worrying about homicide detectives snooping around, he decided to make her overdose.

He kept giving her more and more crack to smoke and made her take bigger and bigger hits until finally, her eyes glazed over. She clutched her heart and dropped onto the filthy concrete floor.

They stepped away from her as her body convulsed and foam came out of her mouth.

When he was sure she was dead, Gerard made Leo help him with the corpse.

They carried her up the stairs, and out to the sidewalk.

Fortunately, the sun wasn't out yet, and no one was around, so they brought Gianna's corpse a few doors down and threw it on top of an old broken sofa that someone had thrown out with the garbage.

Leo went one way and Gerard went the other way.

All the way home, Gerard's heart was pounding. He hoped no one saw them dump the body.

CHAPTER 56

Angelo's beeper went off a few times after he dropped off Frank in Bay Ridge. When he checked it, there were two numbers, his mother's, and his uncle's. He wasn't going to stop and call them from a payphone just to tell them that he couldn't find his sister and she was probably out there somewhere smoking crack and getting fucked by god knows who. He'd be home soon enough to deliver the bad news in person.

He wanted to keep searching for her, but he was exhausted, and he knew Frank was right about getting a different car.

The sun was just coming out when he pulled into his driveway and got out of the car.

He was surprised to see Uncle Larry's Cadillac in front of the house.

When he went inside, his mother was crying hysterically and his uncle had his arm around her. Angelo was shocked to see that his uncle also had tears in his eyes.

Uncle Larry mumbled, "The police found your sister."

Angelo felt sick to his stomach when he realized what his uncle was about to say next.

"She was already dead when they found her."

The hair on the back of Angelo's neck stood as a wave of heat came over his body and then tears ran down his face. How could she be dead? He had just seen her.

There was a knock at the front door. Uncle Larry answered it. His girlfriend was there, also crying. She came in and hugged Angelo's mother. "I'm so sorry."

Uncle Larry wiped his tears then said, "We have to go identify the body."

Angelo felt as if he were dreaming. His mind was numb. He didn't want to leave his mother in that condition, but at least she wasn't alone.

He followed his uncle out the door and into his white Cadillac.

They were both silent as Uncle Larry drove to the morgue.

Inside the gray cold building, a coroner in white rolled a body out of the wall and pulled back the sheet.

It was Gianna. Her cold dead flesh reminded Angelo of when his father died.

Uncle Larry handled all the paperwork then they drove downtown to see his old friend who owned and operated a funeral parlor. The same funeral parlor where Angelo's father was laid out just six years earlier. Everything about it reminded Angelo of his father's funeral. Now his sister would join their father in the afterlife.

Angelo's mind went back to his heartbroken mother as Uncle Larry spoke to his friend about the upcoming funeral.

CHAPTER 57

After spending the evening resting and suffering from his afternoon radiation session, Agent Cortes got a call from Agent Wicker. "How are you feeling?"

Agent Cortes tried to sound stronger than he really was, but he was sure he wasn't fooling anyone. "That depends on what you're gonna tell me. Something good I hope."

Wicker didn't answer.

Cortes asked, "Something bad?"

"The coke the cops took from Leo is gone. Disappeared into thin air. The paperwork is missing too and no one seems to know anything."

Cortes said, "There's a dirty cop."

"Now what?"

"I might be running a little late tomorrow. I want you to go to Internal Affairs first thing in the morning, as soon as they get in, and see if any other evidence has disappeared that way and if they have anyone on their radar that might interest us."

"If you need to stay home tomorrow, I can keep in touch with you by phone."

"Let's see how I feel."

They ended the call, then Cortes lay down on the sofa and turned on the TV.

When the phone rang, he jumped up and felt a rush of blood to his head. He answered.

A man's voice asked, "Cortes?"

Agent Cortes tried his best to speak loud enough. "Who's calling?"

"Detective Zaragoza."

Cortes coughed and sat down on the chair next to the phone. "How can I help you, Detective?"

Zaragoza said, "I think I can help *you*. I heard about your missing evidence."

"Oh, jeez. Don't tell me the entire NYPD knows."

"No. No. Don't worry. Internal Affairs told me."

Agent Cortes' mind started racing with possibilities. "Why would internal affairs contact you?"

"I suspected a beat cop at my old precinct of shaking down dealers, and possibly using the stuff himself, so I went to Internal Affairs about it. And now your evidence just happens to go missing in that same precinct."

"And what made you suspect this cop?"

"I still have snitches around there who come to me now and then when they're desperate for money or when they have information they know will be valuable. There are rumors of the suspected cop entering and leaving a building with a high volume of drug activity. On a daily basis. Sometimes twice a day."

Agent Cortes felt hopeful. If he could find a dirty cop, especially one who's an addict, he could probably flip him and get closer to the Ghost.

After ending the call and dragging himself into the bedroom, Cortes realized that even if he did finally find the Ghost after all this time that there was always the chance of some pricy lawyers getting him off. Then Cortes would have died a defeated man.

He knew that if and when he did get the Ghost, he would have to kill him on the spot.

CHAPTER 58

Angelo hadn't slept all day. Anger, adrenaline, and cocaine kept him wide-awake.

After his uncle had dropped him off at home earlier, Angelo took his mother to her cousin's house in Long Island where she'd have plenty of company. He would have stayed with her, but he had a score to settle.

When he returned to Brooklyn, Angelo went to his connection who hooked him up with a little gray Volvo with fake registration and New Jersey plates. He then went to visit another connection where he bought a snake charmer – a cute little sawed-off shotgun with two barrels.

Back at home, Angelo parked the Volvo inside the garage so no one could see it then he went into the house and ate a couple of cold meatballs that were leftover from Sunday. There was still time, so he lied down on the sofa in the living room and took a long nap.

He woke up in a cold sweat, dreaming of murder.

Angelo drank some soda, and then took another little sniff before walking out the door with his guns and plenty of ammo, and of course, a pair of gloves.

Outside, the sun was already long gone and the temperature had dropped.

He didn't pick up Frank that night because he didn't want his friend implicated in what he was about to do.

When Angelo arrived at the street where he'd killed Juan Carlo, no one recognized him in the Volvo. He pulled up at the same spot and once again saw the guy who had shot at him approaching the car with another guy.

Angelo cocked the snake charmer, stepped out of the car, and blasted the two men in front of him. The sound of the shotgun echoed off the buildings and filled the entire block as the two men were propelled backward.

He turned to see a few people running away and fired the second shot in their direction, not even knowing if he got anyone. The feel of the blast was intoxicating and addictive.

Back in the Volvo, Angelo peeled out, running over the bodies just in case they weren't completely dead.

He sped around the corner and turned down another side street.

There was a group of people on the corner, Angelo had no idea who they were, but it didn't matter anymore. The lethal combination of steroids and cocaine turned his blood into acid. There was no more human compassion. He whipped out his Beretta and began to pick them off one by one.

After unloading the pistol on his unsuspecting victims, he sped down the street and around the corner where he reloaded both guns.

A cop car with its sirens blaring zoomed toward him. Angelo cocked the shotgun, ready to kill the cops, even though he knew that that would make his uncle have no choice but to turn his back on him. And it could possibly mean the end of his life right there, but Angelo didn't care. Nothing mattered.

He waited in the Volvo with the lights off and the snake charmer pointed out the window. His heart was pounding and his breathing was erratic.

Fortunately, the cop kept going. He zipped right past him and then sped around the corner onto the street where Angelo had just been.

Angelo exhaled, then rolled the Volvo forward with its lights still off until he was a few blocks away.

While trying to control his breathing, he turned the lights back on and headed up another side street.

When he arrived at the corner, another dealer approached his car. A big truck roared as it passed on the avenue in front of him. Angelo whipped out his pistol and fired two shots into the man's chest as the truck going by masked the sound.

A chubby guy on the corner, whom Angelo assumed had to be the lookout, tried to run away, but Angelo fired a few shots in his direction. He knew he hit him because the guy went down. He wasn't sure if he killed him, and he didn't have time to make sure, because sirens were beginning to come from all directions.

Angelo drove back down one block to 2nd Avenue. He hated to give up his trusty Beretta, but he had no choice but to leave both of the guns in the car and then knock over a five-gallon red gas can that was already in the back seat and torch the car. The flames increased in size instantly.

He hurried up the block as fast as he could without running, then continued, crossing under the expressway and heading up a residential street to 4th Avenue.

On foot, he continued, all the way up to Bay Ridge while sweat dripped down the back of his shirt.

While passing an entrance to the R-train, Angelo considered taking the subway, but then decided he'd be better off walking. It would take forever, but at least there were more places to run if he was cornered.

When he was a few blocks away from Frank's house, he used a payphone to call him.

CHAPTER 59

When Gerard woke up to an early morning phone call from his aunt that his two cousins had been killed by a shotgun blast on the street, he had a feeling it was Angelo.

Gerard first called Leo and got him out of bed, then they met at one of their hideouts in Park Slope, a second-floor apartment above a fruit stand that was used to cook crack and bag it up.

By the time he got there, he learned that another of his dealers and a lookout were killed on the next block as well as a group of innocent bystanders.

Of course, there was no way of Angelo knowing that they made Gianna overdose on purpose. He was probably just going after every crack dealer he could find. Gerard knew because he would have done the same thing. And like himself, he knew the only way to stop Angelo would be to put him in his grave.

Gerard had called the top members of his gang and they met at the Park Slope cookhouse. He trusted them for the most part, but he never trusted his gang enough to know everything. He told them about Gianna but said she overdosed accidentally on their stuff. Then he made Angelo sound like a primitive beast who wanted to kill every crack dealer to avenge the death of his sister. He said to his gang, "We didn't start this war . . . but we have to finish it."

And with that, every member of the 3rd Avenue Ghosts was hunting for Angelo.

CHAPTER 60

Agent Cortes woke up the next morning vomiting. Although he had slept through most of the night, he was still tired and weak. Once again, he considered giving up. He had plenty of sick days accumulated that he could use rather than going out on permanent disability, and while his worn-out old body was begging for a break, his stubborn mind made him push on.

After getting the news yesterday about the missing evidence, Cortes decided to cancel his afternoon radiation appointment and get some work done. He called the office and left a message for Agent Wicker, telling him to meet him at Police Plaza after he finished with Internal Affairs.

As always, Agent Cortes sat in traffic on his way into Manhattan, inching through the Holland tunnel, and then picking up speed momentarily as he took the west side down and then came back up on the east side taking the streets rather than the FDR Drive.

The NYPD Internal Affairs office was located on Hudson Street near where Cortes had just entered Manhattan, but he'd already instructed Wicker to go there, so Cortes decided to make efficient use of the little time he had left on Earth to investigate the records of Officer Duffy, the cop that Detective Zaragoza suspected of being dirty.

Just after the Brooklyn Bridge entrance ramps was an area of old limestone government buildings adorned with huge columns, small statues, and gothic arches.

Other than the park that housed the ancient city hall building, the area didn't have much greenery.

Cortes pulled up to a metal donut cart and bought a cup of coffee and a buttered roll, which he nibbled and sipped on while driving around the block.

Hidden behind Borough Hall, a forty-story white ornate building with a gilded statue of a crowned woman holding a shield and a leaf branch stood a thirteen-story rectangular red brick building known as Police Plaza, the main headquarters of the NYPD.

Agent Cortes drove up the back way and had to show his DEA badge at the guard booth before he was allowed to enter and park in the five-story red brick garage.

Inside the building, he signed in, placed his gun in a locker, and took the key with him before going through a metal detector. He then headed down a short hallway to the elevator, which he took down to the first basement level where the records department was located.

The clerk seemed happy to help a DEA agent when Agent Cortes showed his badge and identification.

He waited while the clerk disappeared behind the huge stacks of metal file cabinets in the giant gray room behind him.

After at least ten minutes, the clerk returned with a folder.

Cortes signed for the folder and then sat on a hard bench out in the hall while reading Officer Duffy's file. He tried to concentrate on what he was reading rather than on the fact he was having a hard time keeping down the cup of coffee and buttered roll that he had a few minutes earlier.

After a while, his head began to spin, so he took breaks from reading and closed his eyes now and then. He noticed people staring at him when they passed.

He knew he'd have to get permission from another officer to make complete copies of the records, but he didn't have time for extra red tape, so he just jotted down the most important information in his notepad, then thanked the clerk when he returned the files.

Downstairs, Agent Wicker was there, waiting by the parking garage in their government-issued gray van. He asked, "What do you want to do with your car?"

"I'll get it later." Agent Cortes got into the van.

Wicker asked, "You don't want to drive?"

"Not today. What did you find out?"

"Internal Affairs is looking into the complaint. They drug tested Duffy and he came out negative. They already checked his financials and he seems to be broke. So if he is on the take, he's blowing it all on something."

Cortes said, "Or he's saving all the money somewhere for when he needs to disappear."

"That's possible. But for some reason, I have a feeling he's not our man. Oh . . . did you hear about what happened last night under the Gowanus?"

"What happened?"

Wicker answered, "Four members of the 3rd Avenue Ghosts were killed, and a few other people who had nothing to do with the gang were killed. The cops found a sawed-off shotgun and a Beretta in a burning car on 2nd Avenue. No prints. Maybe your Ghost has resurfaced."

"Not his style. Too reckless. And why would he gun down his own people in the street like that when he could have easily lured them to a private location? And why the innocent bystanders?"

"Anyway, I gave the homicide detectives my pager number and told them to call as soon as they have something." Wicker started up the engine then turned to Cortes. "You sure you're up to this? You look terrible."

"I'm fine. Let's just go."

Now that the city had reached its busiest time, it took almost thirty minutes just driving around the block to get back to the entrance ramp for the Brooklyn Bridge.

They spent another hour crawling across the bridge and the Belt Parkway before finally reaching Sheepshead Bay, a residential neighborhood in Brooklyn with six-story apartment buildings on the avenues and two-story houses on tree-lined streets in between.

All the way there, Cortes thought about who could be responsible for the killings last night.

When they arrived at Officer Duffy's two-family detached house, they knocked on the door and then showed their ID's to the skinny woman who answered the door with a half-burnt cigarette hanging from her mouth.

She was obviously flirting with Agent Wicker when she said, "Oh, please. Come in. Let me get you something. Coffee, tea, me?" She had a raspy laugh.

Agent Cortes coughed and shook his head. "Nothing. Thank You. We're looking for Officer Duffy."

"Why would the DEA be looking for my husband?"

Wicker replied, "We need to talk to him about an arrest he made. Is he home?"

"Home? He's supposed to be working. You telling me he's not?"

Cortes didn't want an angry wife getting to Officer Duffy before they did, so he glanced at his notepad and lied, "Wait a minute . . . today is Wednesday. Right? We made a mistake . . . he is working today. Sorry to bother you, Mrs. Duffy." He couldn't tell by the look on her face if she believed him or not, but he didn't want to waste any more time than necessary. "We better get going now."

Agent Wicker followed Cortes back to the van and then asked, "You still want me to drive?"

Cortes nodded. "I have an address Zaragoza gave me. A known crack spot." He showed his notepad to Wicker.

"Let's go." Wicker took the Belt Parkway to Bay Ridge then took 3rd Avenue all the way down to where the Gowanus Expressway turned and took over the landscape.

They stopped at a building on the corner of a residential street.

Two suspicious characters standing out front scurried away when they saw the gray van.

At night, these streets would be crawling with dealers, but it was barely lunchtime.

Sitting in the van, Agent Cortes rifled through his notepad and retrieved a small picture of Officer Duffy in uniform. He had black hair with blue eyes and a strong jaw and cheekbone and could have easily been a model or a movie star rather than a cop.

Agent Wicker said, "If we're going to be knocking on every apartment door, I think we should request some back-up."

"Are you scared?"

"Instead of asking me if I'm scared . . . I should be asking you if you have a death wish."

"And what would you suggest?"

"Let's wait a little bit. We'll park across the street on the corner where we can blend in with those trucks at the lumberyard. This is definitely the building Zaragoza told you about . . . right?"

Agent Cortes coughed, nodded, and then said, "And you think he'll come here because he lied to his wife about working today."

"I still don't believe he's our man, but if he does come to this building as often as you say, there has to be a reason."

Cortes was too tired to argue, not to mention drudging up and down the stairs of a five-story building without an elevator. "Let's wait then."

Wicker went around the block then came back up the avenue and parked half-on the sidewalk next to another van that was parked the same way. A man driving a forklift glanced over at the gray government van before continuing to unload palettes of boxes from a big truck parked around the corner on the side street.

Agent Cortes thought about his missed appointment. On one hand, he was hopeful that radiation and chemotherapy might cure him, but on the other hand, he knew the odds were against him, and he didn't have much to live for anyway. He didn't even realize he was falling asleep until Wicker woke him up.

"He's there."

Cortes peeked out the tinted window to see Officer Duffy in civilian clothes on the sidewalk across the street.

The off-duty cop strolled around the corner to the entrance of the building in question, and then scanned the area before going inside.

Agent Wicker started the van and crossed the avenue where he parked directly in front of the building entrance.

The sun was blindingly bright.

After about thirty minutes, Officer Duffy came back out of the building and looked around before strolling down the street passing three-story stone-faced row houses.

Cortes tried to keep up with Wicker as they got out of the van and intercepted Officer Duffy. They showed their credentials.

Agent Wicker asked, "What were you doing in that building?"

"I was just checking in on an old friend. I've already been questioned by internal affairs. They thought I was using drugs. I passed their test. And why is the DEA here now bothering me? I'm clean. If I was dealing you think I'd be taking the bus all the way here?"

Agent Cortes said, "We're here because of our evidence that disappeared in your precinct."

"And I'm your only suspect? Are you kidding me?"

Wicker said, "I can't speak for my partner, but I don't believe you have anything to do with drugs. But your name came up and we have to rule you out. And the only way to rule you out is to get the truth out of you."

"I told you the truth. I'm here checking on a friend."

Wicker asked, "Is your friend that beautiful brunette with a nice rack that was just watching us from her window?"

Agent Cortes looked up, but he must have been too late because he didn't see her. He was impressed by Wicker's observations though.

Officer Duffy pleaded, "Please. I'm married. She's married."

Cortes assured him, "We're not in the business of ruining marriages. But she will have to corroborate your story."

Officer Duffy looked around and then agreed.

They entered the building. Cortes panted as he trailed behind the two healthy men on their way up the musty graffiti-covered staircase to the third floor.

Duffy knocked on the apartment door. "It's me, baby."

She opened the door. "What . . . who are they?"

Cortes and Wicker showed their credentials.

Officer Duffy explained, "I wouldn't do this baby, but these guys are DEA, and if we don't talk to them they're gonna take us both in for questioning."

Cortes was happy Duffy was smart enough to try to convince her to talk.

"They're not going to say anything about us. They don't care about our personal lives. But if we don't cooperate . . . then everyone will find out about us anyway."

Agent Cortes said, "I understand your concerns, Mam. But a serious crime has been committed, and I need to be sure you and Officer Duffy are not involved."

She looked them over, sighed, and then she finally said, "Okay. We're fucking. Is that what you want to hear? Can you go now please?"

Agent Cortes said, "Just as soon as we're sure you don't have a drug dealing den here."

"Are you fucking kidding me? You're not ripping my house apart."

Duffy assured her, "They're not gonna touch anything baby." He turned to the two agents and said, "Right? You just want to take a quick look."

"That's all we need." Replied Agent Wicker. "Just a quick look. No touching."

She stepped out of the doorway, and with her hand extended, she invited them in.

The three men stepped inside. A baby was sleeping in a crib in the living room while something boiled on the stove in the kitchenette. The refrigerator door was full of report cards and drawings by small children and there was a stack of newspapers in the corner.

It was easy to see how frequent visits to his mistress who lived in a drug-ridden building could lead people to believe Duffy was a dirty cop, but like Wicker, Cortes didn't believe Duffy wasn't their man. And standing in front of such an incredibly sexy woman, Cortes could understand how any man would enter the lake of fire just for a glimpse of her. And he knew from experience that her sassy attitude probably meant she was a great fuck.

After leaving Officer Duffy and his hot mistress, they went up to 5th Avenue where they ate a late lunch at McDonald's and then Cortes threw up in the bathroom.

Wicker said, "You look whiter than before. Maybe you should call it a day."

"I'm fine. Let's get down to the courthouse."

Wicker drove downtown to the Brooklyn courts and dropped Cortes off before parking the van.

Cortes hurried into the building as an unexpected rain shower drenched the sidewalks.

Inside the big crowded building, Cortes asked the clerk about the judge he was there to see and the clerk told him he'd have to wait.

He waited on a bench in the hall next to the judge's office while lawyers marched back and forth with files in their hands dodging people who were reading directories and dockets on bulletin boards.

Wicker came in soon after and sat next to him. "Judge is busy?"

Cortes was feeling dizzy again. He nodded, then said, "I'm going to close my eyes for a few minutes. Let me know when that door opens." He closed his eyes and wished he could sleep. He could still hear the hustle and bustle going on around him, but he was able to slip into a semi-sleep state that made him feel a little more relaxed.

He knew that more than an hour had passed because he glanced at his watch when Wicker shook his arm.

A fat pink-faced judge was coming out of his office.

Cortes tried to speak normally but was only able to get out a little more than a whisper. "Your honor. Excuse me."

Wicker said it louder, "Your honor."

The fat judge turned to the two men who were both now on their feet.

Cortes cleared his throat before saying, "I'm Agent Cortes. I filed for the warrants earlier."

"Yes. I almost forgot." The judge re-opened his office door and went inside.

The two agents followed him in. The office was spacious and elegant. Law books filled a bookcase while pictures of distinguished people hung from the walls.

"I already signed the one for the kid. It covers his house and the car registered to him." The judge handed them some papers. "As I understand, it was his cocaine that is now missing. Correct?"

Cortes nodded.

Wicker said, "Yes, your honor."

The judge continued, "And yet you want me to give you warrant to bug his cousin just because he paid his bail?"

Cortes struggled to speak. "We have reason to believe he is one of the leaders of the gang."

The judge ruffled through a small stack of papers on his desk. "I don't see any paperwork here on that. I hope you're not asking me to give you a warrant on a hunch."

Neither Cortes nor Wicker answered.

CHAPTER 61

After arriving at Frank's house, Angelo had washed up and then called a car service to take him home.

All the way home, his heart was still pounding and his blood was still full of adrenaline. Once in the house, he checked to make sure all the doors and windows were secure before trying to get some sleep.

His mind wasn't ready to rest yet, so he turned on the TV and stared at it all night.

When the morning sun began to rise, that's when he finally fell asleep, but not for long. He slept on and off, always waking up sweaty with a pounding heart, dreaming of the people he'd just killed, and dreaming that he was running from the police. Some of the dreams were just flames, probably because of the car he had left burning, or possibly signifying that he would one day burn in hell. Once again, thanks to the steroids, the dreams were vivid and felt real. The same dreams even continued sometimes after waking up and falling back asleep.

It was early afternoon before he finally gave up on sleeping and made a pot of coffee. He thought about taking another sniff to really wake him up, but he didn't want to go to the funeral parlor that evening high.

The leftovers in the refrigerator had been there for a few days and didn't smell so good, so he threw out the old food and made himself a peanut butter sandwich. There was no milk to wash it down with so he took a gulp from a two-liter soda bottle and then proceeded to the shower.

Before getting dressed, Angelo called his mother's cousin in Long Island, but his mother was busy getting ready so he said he'd call back later.

Very few people knew what had really happened to Gianna. Angelo and his uncle told people that Gianna had died of an aneurism. They felt like it would shame the family if everyone knew she had been smoking crack and died of an overdose.

At the funeral home, Angelo sat up front with his mother and his uncle as everyone stopped at the coffin to make the sign of the cross and then tell the family how they were sorry for their loss. Family, friends, and strangers came to show their respects. Even the boss and underboss of the family were there.

The beige carpets, wood furniture, and the hundreds of flower bouquets reminded Angelo of his father's funeral. Even the distant music was the same.

CHAPTER 62

Gerard's people had been out searching for Angelo and quickly learned what funeral parlor Gianna's wake would be at. He remembered what Leo had said about Angelo's family being mafia, so he decided to hire an independent professional Hitman, Cheo.

When Gerard got a page from Cheo, he was expecting a code on his beeper, *999*, meaning that Angelo was dead and Cheo was ready for the rest of his payment. But instead, the number on the beeper read, *411*. Gerard wondered if Cheo needed information or had information for him. He texted him back with a *39*, which meant they would meet at the donut shop on 39th Street.

Inside the donut shop, the fake-wood paneled walls were scratched and gouged and the old tile floor was dull and scuffed. A Michael Jackson song played over the speakers hanging above the counter.

Gerard sat at the counter next to Cheo, a tall fat black Puerto-Rican with the face of a bulldog. He ordered a cup of coffee and pretended not to know the Hitman next to him. After the girl gave him his coffee and a roll with butter, Gerard spoke quietly. "What's up?"

Cheo kept his usually loud voice to a minimum when he said, "I found him. That was the easy part. But there's a problem."

Gerard stirred the milk and sugar into his coffee.

Cheo continued, "There's about a hundred mafia guys there. I know because I did jobs for a couple of them. Two cops were sitting in an unmarked car watching the funeral . . . and there was a suspicious panel truck across the street . . . probably FBI." Cheo slid a white paper envelope full of cash to Gerard, "I can't do this one for you. Sorry, bro"

CHAPTER 63

When Agent Cortes woke up the next morning, he was too sick and weak to get out of bed, so he left a message for Wicker that he would not be coming in, then he went back to sleep for a couple more hours.

The second time he woke up, he was feeling a little better, but when he realized he only had thirty minutes to get to his appointment, he had no choice but to skip taking a shower and drive down to the medical complex with just a fresh spray of deodorant under his arms.

He almost fell asleep again on the bed as the big mechanical arms delivered radiation to his torso.

Afterword, his back was stiff when getting off the bed, so the technicians helped him to his feet.

When he noticed his reflection in a shiny metal plate, he realized that he was no longer the star of the high school football team, he was just a sick weak old man.

Back at home, Cortes saw his answering machine blinking. He listened to the two messages.

The first message was one he'd missed earlier that morning. A reminder of his radiation therapy appointment.

The second message was from Agent Wicker, telling him to return the call.

Cortes called the office and got Wicker on the phone. "So what happened today?"

"They planted the microphone in Leo's car early this morning while it was parked in the lot."

Cortes asked, "And what did you get so far?"

"A lot of loud music and an argument in Spanish with some girl. The translator said they were fighting because the girl suspected Leo of having another girl on the side."

Agent Cortes knew how dangerous jealousy could be and he wondered if he would be able to get the girl to flip on Leo. He was still hoping for a smoking gun, but at least he knew he had some options. Cortes said, "I'm going to lay down a bit. Call me if you come up with anything useful."

After getting off the phone, Cortes went into the bathroom to vomit, but there was nothing inside of him except stomach acids.

Once again, he thought about the Ghost of 3rd Avenue. Of course, there would be more dealers to replace the Ghost. As long as people wanted drugs, someone would be there to supply them. But Cortes worried that since he'd already put so much of his heart, as well as his reputation, into this case, that if he didn't catch him, he would die a failure.

CHAPTER 64

When Cara hadn't seen Angelo or Frank in the gym for the past couple of days, she thought it was because of the fight. The police had been there after the fight, but everyone said they hadn't seen anything. Cara wasn't there when the police came because after seeing how shook up she was, Big Mike had taken her home.

She wasn't sure what she would say to Angelo when he eventually did come into the gym, but she hoped it didn't become so uncomfortable that she'd have to quit working there.

That morning, Big Mike called Cara at home and told her that Angelo's sister had died of an aneurism. He said that he was in Connecticut the day before when he heard the bad news so he had already missed the first day of the wake. He told Cara that if she wanted to go to the funeral parlor that evening with him and his girlfriend that he could have someone take her place at the gym and he would still pay her for the day. She agreed, and although she said she didn't want to take the money, Big Mike insisted.

Of course, she knew she couldn't make a life with Angelo, but she still had strong feelings for him and couldn't ignore the fact that his sixteen-year-old sister had just died.

She put on a pair of black pants and a black shirt and then told her mother where she was going.

At first, her mother looked as if she were about to argue, but when she told her about Angelo's dead sister, Cara's mother lightened up and gave her permission to go.

Big Mike and his supermodel girlfriend picked Cara up at her house.

When they arrived at the funeral home downtown, Cara said, "I'd like to stay here in the back for a little while if you don't mind."

Big Mike replied, "Listen . . . if you don't want to stay the whole time, let me know. I can bring you home and I'll come back."

Cara replied, "Thank you, but you don't have to do that. I'll take car service home later."

Big Mike took out a twenty-dollar bill and tried to give it to her. "Take this for the car . . . in case you don't want to wait for me."

"I have money on me." Replied Cara.

Big Mike insisted, "Take it. Please."

Cara sat alone in a big chair against the side wall while Big Mike and Lulu approached Gianna's coffin.

Soft classical music was barely audible in the background and the dim lights made the atmosphere feel comfortable and soothing. Cara noticed a few people who she had met at the barbeque and she hoped that none of them would recognize her.

After about an hour of fighting with herself about going up to the front to see Angelo and his mother, she noticed Angelo getting up. He made his way down the opposite side to the door and took a cigarette from another man. She turned away so he wouldn't notice her as he went out of the room and into the hall.

Cara knew he'd be out there at least long enough to smoke the cigarette, so she stood up and headed to the front with her head down.

She knelt in front of the coffin. Gianna was young and beautiful. Cara's eyes filled with tears as she looked up at the crucifix on the wall and gave herself the sign of the cross.

Before turning around to face Angelo's mother, Cara tried to swallow and cleared her throat.

"I'm sorry for your loss." She knelt down and kissed Angelo's mother on the cheek, then shook the hands of the two old women sitting next to her. As she made her way back to her big empty chair, Cara realized that Angelo's mother didn't seem to recognize her.

She sat alone once again against the side wall, and when Angelo came back in with his uncle, Cara had the overwhelming feeling to go to him and embrace him and tell him how sorry she was about his sister, but she didn't. She just stayed there in silence as Angelo and his uncle made their way to the front of the room and sat down in the second row behind the women.

Cara saw a few of the older men from the barbeque gawking at her, and she didn't want to have to answer any questions about her and Angelo, so she got up and left.

Tears flooded her eyes as she hurried out of the air-conditioned building and into the sweltering humidity.

She didn't know where she was going. She just started to walk.

When she saw a yellow taxi double-parked on the next block, she peeked inside to see that the driver wasn't there. A man's voice asked, "Can I help you?"

Cara turned around to see a man holding a paper bag with a grease stain. She said, "I need to go to Dyker Heights."

"Get in." The man got behind the wheel, started up the engine, and turned on the meter.

Cara got in the back seat but then turned to glance out the back window at the funeral parlor as they drove away from it. She felt terrible for not talking to Angelo.

CHAPTER 65

After managing to keep down some bread and butter, Agent Cortes turned on the TV and tuned to the Mets vs. Braves game.

When his phone rang, he didn't feel like getting off the sofa to answer it, but he had a feeling it was Agent Wicker, since no one other than telemarketers ever called him.

He struggled to stand because of the pain in his lower back, but he made it to the phone.

Wicker said, "Everything is in place. When Leo was out, the team got into his apartment and planted three bugs. One in the phone, one in the living room, and one in the bedroom."

"I assume that if you had a smoking gun that you would have started with that."

"No smoking gun yet. Just Leo's little sister getting home from school and then his mother getting home and cooking dinner while listening to music. I have a feeling we'll get more out of his car if we get anything."

"If we get anything? Have some faith, my young friend."

"How are you feeling?"

Cortes didn't like sympathy. "Better. I might come in for a couple of hours tomorrow morning before my radiation."

CHAPTER 66

Gerard had hoped to be out of court by lunchtime, but he should have known better.

That evening, as he left the old limestone court building, he paged Leo from a payphone on the corner and when Leo called back, Gerard told him to come downtown and pick him up.

The funeral parlor where Gianna was laid out was within walking distance of the courts, but Gerard didn't want to be out in the open like that. He couldn't just walk in there.

He stood there waiting for over thirty minutes. When Leo finally arrived, Gerard asked, "What the hell?"

"There's traffic. It's the middle of rush hour."

"Rush hour." He got into Leo's little red BMW and they headed up Court Street.

The street narrowed and then neighborhood changed from high-rise office buildings and old government buildings to three and four-story brick buildings with storefronts and wide sidewalks lined with flourishing trees.

The funeral parlor was in a busy area of cars, buses, and bicycles. The sidewalk outside was full of people and trucks were double-parked making last minute deliveries.

Leo cruised by nice and slow, glancing in his rearview mirror. "There's a cop car a couple blocks back, coming this way."

"Go around the block then."

As Leo made the turn, he noticed the suspicious panel truck that Cheo was talking about. Leo said, "Look there . . . at that truck."

Now that Gerard had assessed the situation for himself, he agreed with everyone else that it couldn't be done there. He knew he'd have to wait.

When Leo made the turn onto the next side street, a car pulled away from a parking meter. Gerard said, "Take that spot."

Leo pulled into the parking spot that had just become vacant. "Don't tell me we're going in there."

"Just walk by. Check out the days and the times on that sign by the door."

Leo got out of the car then strolled up the block to Court Street where he turned the corner and disappeared.

As Gerard sat there, waiting for Leo to return, the same cop car cruised down the avenue.

After a few minutes, Leo came back with two cans of soda in his hand.

"One block made you thirsty?"

"I couldn't just walk by there and then turn around and walk back. You know how suspicious that would look? I had to do something." He handed a soda to Leo.

"I don't want that. What did the sign say?"

"Tomorrow they take her to the cemetery."

CHAPTER 67

All night, Cara dreamt of Gianna's cold corpse.

When she woke up the next morning, she realized it was the first night that she didn't dream about the evil in Angelo's eyes when he pummeled that man almost to death.

She went into the tidy living room to find her mother drinking a cup of coffee while watching the morning news. A laundry basket full of folded clothes sat on the floor next to her.

Cara had been going back and forth in her mind about going to Gianna's burial, and when she heard the newscasters joking about bad luck because it was Friday the 13th, Cara wondered if that were a sign of things to come. What if there was more violence? A mob hit or another fight. Was she just being ridiculous?

Then she thought about how her brothers would feel if she had died at such a young age. She would hope they had as many people around them as possible to comfort them.

Her mother asked, "So . . . are you going today?"

"I don't know."

"What did he say when he saw you last night?"

"He didn't see me. I waited for him to go out for a smoke before I went up to the coffin. Did I do wrong?"

"Sometimes there's no right or wrong, Sweetie. Just what we feel."

Cara cried.

Her mother hugged her.

Finally, Cara said, "I'm gonna go."

"I'll drive you."

Cara didn't have any more black pants, so she put on a black dress and covered her bare legs with black stockings.

Her mother didn't dress for the funeral because she planned on staying in the car. She didn't know anyone there and she always hated funerals anyway.

They entered Greenwood cemetery on 5th Avenue, through the ancient Gothic main entrance, which consisted of two brownstone arches, three towers, a chapel, and an office. The center tower featured a clock and a spire and was taller than the other two towers, one on either side of the arches.

Inside the cemetery, there were enormous mausoleums and extravagant tombstones and statues, as well as hundreds of traditional plots.

"I'll be at the bottom of that hill, sweetie." Cara's mother dropped her off at the group of people then drove out of sight.

Cara stood in the back, behind the crowd, and spotted Angelo with his mother and uncle directly in front of the open grave. The priest stood behind the coffin and said prayers while everyone wept.

Finally, they threw flowers into the grave, on top of the coffin, and then the first shovel of dirt was thrown in.

Cara was already crying, but when she heard Angelo's mother wailing, she lost it.

CHAPTER 68

As the dirt landed on the coffin and slowly rose to the top of the grave, Angelo felt the emptiness in his heart growing. It was the first time since he had seen Gianna's corpse in the morgue that he didn't have revenge in his heart. He felt defeated. He knew he could hunt and kill more crack dealers—he could kill all of them—but that wouldn't change anything. His sister was now in the ground.

After the priest made his final blessing and the grave was full of dirt, Angelo turned around and saw Cara's face instantly among all the others. Maybe she was there to give him another chance. He knew how she felt about his family business and for her, he would give it all up.

He whispered to his mother, "I'll be right back, Ma."

His mother and uncle stood there as other people began to leave.

When he approached Cara, he extended his hand, but to his surprise, she hugged him. He could tell she had been crying but wasn't anymore. Once they embraced, she began to sob. So did he.

After a few moments, they separated and wiped the tears from their eyes.

"I'm so sorry about your sister. I was at the wake yesterday."

"I didn't see you there."

"I know."

Angelo turned to see that his uncle was now walking with his mother and a group of other people toward the cars. He turned back to Cara and said, "Come eat with us. There's a lot of people going. It's not just family."

"No. I couldn't."

Angelo wasn't expecting her to say yes, so he wasn't disappointed. Once again, he thought about telling her about the fight and the steroids, but he knew it wasn't the time or the place.

Cara added, "I'm sorry. I just don't feel comfortable. And besides . . . my mom is here . . . waiting for me in the car."

Angelo remembered that Cara had said her parents didn't like him, and that made his heart feel just a little heavier. He said, "Don't worry about it."

"What about tonight? Dinner. Just to talk."

Her sweet little voice once again made Angelo become overwhelmed with emotion and gave him the slightest sense of hope. His eyes began to tear again and he choked on his own words when he nodded and tried to say yes.

CHAPTER 69

Gerard and Leo had been sitting in Leo's car, in the cemetery, just far away enough to see when the crowd dispersed.

He spotted Angelo hugging a blonde girl while other people got in their cars and drove away.

They followed them to the restaurant where they stayed inside for over two hours.

Leo was getting restless.

Gerard asked, "You got somewhere to go?"

"I just wish they would finish eating already."

When they finally came out of the restaurant, Gerard noticed that Angelo got into his car alone. He already knew where he lived, so he didn't need to follow him. He just wanted to be sure that he'd be alone.

After Angelo drove off and Gerard and Leo headed back up 5th Avenue, Gerard got a page.

Leo asked, "You want me to find a phone?"

"No. Let's just get back. I still have a lot to do."

When Leo dropped Gerard off at home, Gerard instructed, "I'll page you before I go, then again when I need you to pick me up."

CHAPTER 70

Agent Cortes had made it into the office that morning, not as early as he had planned, but he still had enough time to do some paperwork before heading back to New Jersey for his afternoon radiation appointment.

Inside their dull but clean office, Wicker was sitting behind his desk, filling out forms. "Hey. You made it. Good timing. Right now Gerard is in the car with Leo. They were at the cemetery earlier, watching the funeral of some girl that died of an overdose. Now they're spying on the dead girl's family as they eat dinner. Last night they were watching the wake."

"Who is this girl?"

"Gianna Manigritto. Her uncle is a known mobster. A capo in the Profaci family."

Cortes said out loud what he was thinking, "What the hell is going on?"

Wicker replied, "That girl died just a couple of days after Juan Carlo was buried."

"It sounds like you have a theory."

"My Theory? I think someone in that girl's family wanted revenge for her death."

"Are you saying that someone made her overdose on purpose?"

"Possibly. But even if it were accidental . . . I know that I'd go after my sister's supplier if she died of an overdose. I would probably kill every crack dealer I could find."

Cortes assessed the situation in his head and agreed with Wicker, but he wouldn't tell him that.

He wondered if these killings would be enough to bring out the real Ghost once and for all. He also considered the fact that a lunatic on a murderous rampage can be a big help when it comes to getting dealers off the street.

Cortes pretended to disagree with Wicker's theory. "I do like the way you think out of the box. But that theory there . . . it might be a bit of a stretch."

CHAPTER 71

Later that afternoon, Gerard walked down to an auto repair shop between 2nd and 3rd Avenues with a dozen cars parked out front, some of them partially on the sidewalk.

Inside, Gerard shook hands with an older man in the front office, then followed a younger man who had the same face and build as the older man.

They passed through the garage, which smelled of gasoline and grease. Two mechanics in blue overalls were working on the engines of two different cars while salsa music played from an old radio on the workbench.

After going out the back door and into the yard, Gerard had to step around old rusted engine parts, fenders, and wheels that had weeds growing up from between them.

The fence to the next back yard had a hidden area where it was loose. The young man untied two wires and pulled the metal fence back far enough for them to go through to the next backyard, which was only about four feet of cracked old concrete.

The young man opened a padlock to the back door of an old warehouse.

Inside, the huge open space was filled with engines on wooden pallets as well as a huge array of stolen cars. Most of the cars there were too nice and would attract attention. Gerard had already been there the night before and asked for something inconspicuous.

The young man showed Gerard a newly acquired, little beige hatchback, a Chevy Citation. "How's that for inconspicuous?"

Gerard said, "Perfect. But, I just hope I don't get stuck in a dangerous situation."

The young man pointed at a Camaro on cinderblocks with the hood open and nothing under it. "The motor and tranny from that Camaro is in your little car. It's a V8 with some serious balls."

"Really?"

"There wasn't much room in the engine compartment, so if you run it for a long time, it could overheat. And you will have to sweat in there. No space to connect the AC . . . it would have made her overheat for sure anyway. But if you need to get away from somewhere in a snap . . . this little bitch will do it."

"And how much is this gonna cost me?"

The young man responded in broken Spanish, "Only what I paid for the car. Nothing extra. Consider it me doing my part. Just get that bastard."

Gerard got behind the wheel of the little car and started it up. The engine felt powerful.

"The plates are clean. At least they will be for a couple a days." The young man then went out through a small door in the front of the building and a minute later, he rolled up one of the big steel gates.

After quietly rolling the little car out into the street, Gerard drove away from the graffiti-covered building as the young man rolled the gate back down.

He drove the powerful little car to Gravesend, and then drove past Angelo's house and parked up the block near the corner where he could keep an eye on Angelo's car through his rearview mirror.

Cars and trucks went back and forth on the avenue in front of him, but there weren't many people out walking around.

With his gun loaded and the safety off, Gerard sat there, waiting as his heart beat faster, and his hands began to sweat.

CHAPTER 72

After the funeral and lunch at the restaurant, Uncle Larry had driven Angelo's mother back to Long Island so she could stay a few more days with her cousins.

Angelo went home and finally slept peacefully. It was only a few hours, but the entire time, he dreamt of Cara's sweet voice and her sometimes too-loud laugh.

The feeling of his sister's death still loomed over him like a dark cloud, but the thought of Cara was his silver lining. She represented hope.

While Angelo dressed, he wondered which clothes he could wear that would make him look like less of a street thug and more of a potential husband. He opted for a pair of khakis, a long-sleeve button-down shirt, and his Member's Only jacket.

After putting on his Rolex, he went for his pinky ring, but changed his mind and left them both in the jewelry box that had once belonged to his father. The only jewelry he wore was a new Citizen watch that one of his aunts bought him for graduation.

When he picked up Cara at her house that evening, he was five minutes early, and once again, she was waiting for him outside.

She wore a loose-fitting light sweater and gray business pants with her hair in a tight bun. It was obviously an attempt to avoid looking sexy. But it didn't work. She was always sexy.

Angelo noticed Cara's mother peering out the window.

When Cara approached, he got out of the car and opened her door. He didn't try to kiss or hug her, and neither did she.

Inside the car, Angelo changed the station to some easy-listening music, then turned down the volume so they could have a conversation.

Other than small talk, they didn't speak much while driving down 86th Street to 5th Avenue.

Angelo parked at a two-hour meter on the corner and then they awkwardly strolled down the busy sidewalk one block to a Chinese restaurant.

CHAPTER 73

Gerard had almost missed Angelo when he got into his black Lincoln and sped past him.

Staying two to three cars back, he followed Angelo down 86th Street. He had a good shot when Angelo got off the main street and drove through a quiet residential neighborhood to pick up the same blonde girl who was with him at the cemetery earlier, but there were children outside playing on the sidewalk and Gerard could see a woman watching from inside the girl's house. Too many witnesses. He decided to wait.

Gerard then followed them down 86th Street, still staying two to three cars back, and wondering if he should have taken the shot when he had the chance. He had another good shot at one point on 86th Street, but a cop had a car pulled over by the gas station and was writing a ticket. Too close for comfort.

In Bay Ridge, Gerard watched as Angelo and the blonde parked at a meter on 5th Avenue. When Angelo and the blonde got out of the car, Gerard cruised past them.

He watched them enter a Chinese restaurant, then he turned down the next street and came back up 86th Street from the opposite side. He parked his little beige Chevy one block before Angelo's Lincoln.

Once again, Gerard waited with his loaded gun in his hand. This time his heart pounding even harder than before.

Inside the fancy restaurant, Angelo and Cara sat in a booth with red leather seats and white tablecloths. Dim lights illuminated ceramic red dragons on the walls while subtle Chinese music in the background provided for an exotic ambiance. Angelo wanted something as far away from Italian as possible.

He ordered white wine. Cara sipped it but didn't seem crazy about it. He didn't know what he was ordering so he took Cara's advice and ordered some type of chicken with vegetables. At first, they were both still silent as they waited for their food to come.

After a little wine, Angelo pleaded, "I know what you saw of me the other night was . . ." he almost said fucked up, but changed it to, "terrible." He noticed the expression on her face. He knew she didn't want to hear another apology, but Angelo continued, "I'm taking steroids. That's why I got so crazy. I know it doesn't excuse what I did, but I didn't want to go through life knowing that you thought I was naturally that violent. I just had to say it. That's all."

Cara didn't answer, instead, she gulped her wine down in one shot and then poured herself another half glass.

Angelo would have liked to down the entire bottle and order a few more, but that wouldn't have been very gentlemanly. He was surprised at himself for being so pathetic . . . just for a girl. But the angel in front of him wasn't just some girl.

They made more small talk as they ate.

Angelo was pleasantly surprised with his meal.

After they ate, Cara finished off the little bit of wine left in her glass and said, "I'm supposed to tell you that I never wanna see you again." She chuckled, obviously a little buzzed.

Angelo smiled. He wanted to kiss her so bad. He wanted to be stranded with her on a desert island in the middle of nowhere, or on a planet far away from everything.

"Does that mean I have to join another gym?"

"Of course not. We're still friends. Right?"

That's not what he wanted to hear, but at least she no longer was looking at him like a beast. Friends with an angel would be a privilege. He smiled. "Friends."

After paying the bill, Angelo and Cara stepped outside.

He was ready to light up a cigarette when he changed his mind.

They strolled one block back to the car and then he opened the door for her and she got in.

Finally, Gerard saw Angelo and the blonde girl coming out of the restaurant and walking back to Angelo's car. He worried that he'd miss because of how much his hands trembling. He tried to control his breathing and his heart rate while watching Angelo and the girl get into Angelo's Lincoln.

The sidewalks were still full of people and the streets were still full of cars. Not a good place to kill someone. Gerard decided to follow them back to the girl's quiet neighborhood and take Angelo out there, where there wouldn't be so many witnesses.

He started his little car and pulled up slowly, wondering if they might be going somewhere else. Maybe to a movie, or a club, or somewhere for dessert. He might find the perfect place and time to kill Angelo, but then again, he might be squandering his only chance.

Knowing that his license plates would be more dangerous to use with each passing day, and wondering if this would be the only time he could get to Angelo without also having to shoot it out with a bunch of armed gangsters, Gerard wasn't satisfied with his plan of waiting. This was his chance and he was going to take it.

Just as he was ready to pull up next to Angelo's car, a taxi whipped out in front of him and then slammed on its brakes when the light turned red, blocking Angelo's car from pulling out.

Gerard also slammed on his breaks to avoid hitting the taxi in front of him. He wanted to get out and say something to the cab driver, but he controlled himself.

He sat there in his car, still with his gun in his hand, pouring sweat as he waited for the light to turn green.

Sitting next to Angelo in the car, Cara was once again captivated by him. She knew it was partly because of the wine, but she couldn't deny the fact that she was crazy about him. The revelation about his steroid use wasn't something a girl would want to hear, but it did make her wonder if that really was responsible for his behavior. He didn't seem like that type of man, and his eyes did look as if he were possessed that day.

She quickly regained her senses when she thought about her parents.

Angelo started the car and glanced over at Cara. She felt like a little girl in his presence. She glanced down and noticed a spot of food on her sweater. "I spilled something on my sweater."

"There's napkins in the glove compartment."

Cara reached forward to open it and was almost expecting to find a gun or a knife, instead, she saw a jewelry box. She took a napkin from the stack and asked, "New girlfriend?"

"What?" He glanced over at the open glove compartment and said, "What, that? I only got it because I got a good deal on it. I don't know why I kept it. To tell you the truth, I was gonna take it somewhere to sell it."

"What is it?"

"Nothing."

"Was it something for me?" Her heart melted. She took the box out and opened it. Inside was a gold promise ring with two hearts and a diamond in the middle. Her eyes filled with tears.

"I know we only knew each other for a couple weeks . . . I only bought it because I got a good deal on it. I was going to wait and give it to you for a holiday or something. It's just a little thing."

Cara didn't know what came over her but she was happy to blame it on the wine. Her heart burned for him. She jumped on his lap and kissed him as every inch of her flesh tingled.

While kissing Cara's soft delicious lips, Angelo felt a warm feeling in his heart and a sense of hope for the future. She was the one he would marry and have children with. They would buy a house in the suburbs with a white picket fence and live happily ever after.

The red light turned green.

The taxi in front of Gerard moved forward.

Gerard's heart pounded so hard he could hear it.

He pulled up to Angelo's car, leaned toward the open passenger side window, and fired two shots into Angelo's car. The gunshots echoed. Gerard's ears were ringing.

Everyone on the sidewalk either hit the deck or scattered.

In a daze, Gerard stepped on the gas pedal.

The powerful engine roared as he zipped through traffic in the tiny little car and then turned down a side street to get away from any potential witnesses.

Angelo was ripped out of his picket fence fantasy by the sound of two gunshots.

His mind didn't register how close the shots were until he tasted blood in his mouth.

At first, he thought was his blood, but when he pulled his mouth away from Cara's he realized it was her blood, dripping from her mouth while she choked on something.

Her eyes rolled back in her head.

Her body began to convulse.

That's when Angelo noticed blood dripping from a bullet hole in her neck. He felt her soul leaving her body.

CHAPTER 74

After getting away from the area, Gerard dumped the little car on the concrete divider under the Gowanus Expressway between a stack of garbage and a couple of other abandoned cars. He'd had his gloves on the entire time so he wasn't worried about fingerprints. The gun was a throw-away, already hot before he had gotten it, so he threw it into the pile of garbage and then tried to hurry away without appearing guilty.

He was supposed to page Leo to pick him up but didn't want to stop in the little beige car to use the phone. And after he left the car and started walking, he just kept walking, all the way up to 7th Avenue, then down another ten blocks to his apartment building.

As soon as he got home, he washed his trembling hands and tried to catch his breath before going into the kitchen where his wife was warming up his dinner.

The girls were in their room watching cartoons, so Gerard turned on the news and learned that he had missed Angelo and killed his girlfriend instead. The reporters tried to interview Angelo but he wouldn't talk to them. Other people told the reporters what they had seen and heard, and while none of their stories was the same, more than a few people said they had seen a little beige hatchback speeding away. He just hoped the car or the gun couldn't be traced back to him.

Gerard's hands started to tremble again. He noticed his wife staring at him, and although he didn't tell her exactly what was going on, he was sure she had an idea.

CHAPTER 75

Agent Cortes had eaten a small lunch with Agent Wicker before leaving the DEA office to go to his afternoon appointment.

After radiation, he went home to rest and turned on the TV to watch the next game in the Mets Braves series.

He was in the bathroom vomiting up the burger that he had for dinner when his phone rang. He wiped and rinsed his mouth but didn't make it to the phone on time.

Just as he was about to pick it up and page Agent Wicker, the phone rang again. "Hello?"

Wicker said, "You remember my theory about that dead girl? Well, I was right. Someone just tried to kill her brother, but accidentally killed his girlfriend. He's at the precinct giving a statement right now."

Cortes felt dizzy and had to sit down on the chair next to the phone. "So you were right." He wondered who did the shooting. He couldn't see Leo as the murderous type. He wondered if it could have been the Ghost himself. If it was . . . that would be the first time he missed. And although he didn't believe Gerard was the Ghost, Cortes was sure Gerard was one of the highest-ranking members of the gang. Cortes asked Wicker, "Who do you think did it?"

"After listening to those tapes, it sounded to me like Gerard was planning to do it himself."

Cortes lied, "I don't think it was Gerard. Anyway, it's late, and I'm not feeling so well. I'll give you a call tomorrow morning."

After ending the call, Cortes called 411. He already knew the last name of the girl who died. Fortunately, it wasn't a common name, there was only one listed in Brooklyn.

Cortes knew he shouldn't be calling from his own phone, but he had a feeling he wouldn't live long enough to be disciplined anyway.

He called every fifteen minutes but hung up when the answering machine came on.

A couple of hours passed by the time Angelo finally answered his phone. "Hello?"

Cortes cleared his throat and spoke in his loudest possible voice. "The man responsible for your sister's death is the same man responsible for your girlfriend's death."

"Who is this?"

"The enemy of your enemy."

"That supposed to make you my friend?"

"That depends how you look at it. Is anyone listening to your conversation right now?"

Angelo replied, "Just say what you gotta say."

Cortes gave Angelo Gerard's address and apartment number.

"How do you know this?"

"I can't say whether or not he pulled the trigger, but I can say that if he didn't do it himself, it was him who gave the order." Cortes hung up the phone and went back to the sofa where he coughed and coughed and wished for death.

CHAPTER 76

Gerard woke up to the sound of his apartment door being smashed in.

When he realized it wasn't a dream, his first thought was that it was the cops. There were no drugs in his apartment so he wasn't worried about catching any charges, but just in case it wasn't the cops, he reached over to the nightstand where he kept his loaded forty-five. But Gerard was too late. Angelo was standing in his bedroom with a gun of his own.

Angelo fired a shot into Gerard's shoulder just as he grasped his pistol.

Gerard involuntarily dropped his gun. He tried to ignore the excruciating pain in his shoulder while rolling over on top of his screaming wife to shield her from Angelo's bullets, but that also was a futile move.

Angelo fired two shots into her head, instantly silencing her screams.

Without a thought in his mind, Gerard lunged toward Angelo. Angelo fired his gun again.

He didn't feel where the shot penetrated, but Gerard knew he was hit when he tried to make it to his feet but his leg gave out and he fell to the floor. He knew he was a dead man. There was no fighting back now. All he could do was pray.

Angelo kicked Gerard in the face.

Gerard tried to cover his face with his hands but Angelo kept kicking. First getting through his defenses, then when Gerard finally dropped his hands, Angelo's foot busted his nose and teeth.

Finally, Gerard thought about his two daughters sleeping in the next room and when he tried one last time to move, Angelo stomped on his head.

Everything faded to black.

CHAPTER 77

Angelo knew Gerard was already dead, but he kept kicking him in the head until brain matter was exposed. Then he kicked him in the body. He could hear the ribs cracking and wished Gerard was still alive so he could feel it. Angelo kicked the corpse so much that his feet hurt.

Finally, he wiped the sweat from his forehead and was about to leave when he heard the cries of the two little girls in the other bedroom.

He stepped into their little pink room and an array of stuffed animals on a shelf reminded him of his sister. Then he thought about his sister's corpse and his crying mother while the two little girls hugged each other and sobbed. Angelo's eyes filled with tears. The thought of how terrible these little girls' lives would be now after losing both of their parents made him think that he'd be doing them a favor if he killed them too.

Angelo pointed his gun at the two little girls as they cried, finger on the trigger, ready to put them out of their misery, ready to squeeze the trigger—but he couldn't do it.

The sound of sirens outside awoke him from his trance, so he put away his newly acquired gun just in case he'd be needing it again, and then he hurried out of the apartment and down the stairs.

Before getting to the lobby, he could hear people's voices . . . a lot of people. He slipped his sunglasses on and then kept his head down while screaming in a high pitched voice, "He's got a gun! Run!"

The group of people that was gathered in the lobby trampled each other in a panic while trying to get out the front door.

Angelo raced outside in the middle of the crowd and then bolted around the corner where he then slowed his pace to a fast walk until he was at the next block.

He proceeded around the next corner to where his car was parked, then he dropped the gun in the gutter, not worried about prints, as he had never touched it with his bare hands. He had even used gloves when loading it.

On his way back home, he kept glancing into his rearview mirror to make sure he wasn't being followed. He knew he shouldn't have used his own car, but he didn't have time to think after getting that phone call. The only thing he had time for, was to get a gun and get his revenge.

Angelo couldn't even remember how many people he'd killed at that point. And he still didn't feel satisfied. He wanted to kill the whole world.

Crying for Gianna and Cara all the way home, he cursed god for letting them die.

CHAPTER 78

Agent Cortes argued with the receptionist at the radiation center when he canceled his appointment that morning, then he drove to New York and met Agent Wicker at the office.

It was ninety degrees and humid as hell. Cortes had spent most of his life hating the heat, sweating at just the mention of the sun, but now that he was frail and weak from being radiated, the heat made him feel good.

When he arrived at his office, he already had an idea of what to expect.

Agent Wicker declared, "Someone killed Gerard in his bed last night. Killed his wife, too."

"And the kids?" Asked Cortes.

"The kids are traumatized . . . but they're unharmed."

"Thank god."

Wicker asked, "Any theories?"

"Give me a little time to think about it." Cortes was worried that Wicker was suspicious of him, but he tried to act normal. "Maybe we'll get some new info from the bugs on Leo now. You listen yet this morning?"

Wicker stared at Cortes for a moment, then he said, "Leo picked up Gerard's mother and brought her to his apartment. She's there with his mother right now. Other than that . . . there's nothing."

Cortes said, "You know . . . if we got the warrant to bug Gerard's apartment, we would probably know who killed him."

Once again, Wicker stared at Cortes with that suspicious look on his face.

In an attempt of changing the subject, Cortes said, "Let's sign out some petty cash and then get to Brooklyn and talk to whatever resources we have."

"I'll drive." Wicker stood up from behind his desk and headed toward the door.

Outside, they got in the van and Wicker turned on the air conditioner.

As they made their way over the Brooklyn Bridge, Cortes began to tremble from the cold air pumping into his face. He closed the vent on his side, then gazed out the window at downtown Brooklyn as they approached it and then navigated through the busy streets until reaching the beginning of 3rd Avenue. Cortes checked to see if there was another vent open on his side.

Wicker asked, "You cold?"

"I'm fine."

"You look cold." Wicker lowered the air conditioner to the minimum setting. "I'm not giving you mouth to mouth if you pass out."

"Don't worry. I'd rather die."

They both laughed as Wicker continued up 3rd Avenue.

The pager on Wicker's belt beeped and vibrated. He checked it. "It's the office. With a 911."

"Well, pull over."

Cortes stayed in the van while Wicker spoke on a payphone. He knew something was up when Wicker let the phone drop and raced back to the van.

He stepped on the gas and sped up 3rd Avenue. "Merry Christmas in July."

"What?"

"They just got the Ghost on tape . . . in Leo's car."

"Don't fuck with me."

"You were right, but at the same time you were wrong."

"You going to wait for me to die before telling me?"

Wicker didn't wait for the red light, instead, he whipped out the secret siren that they had never used, placed it on the dashboard, and beeped his horn at the same time while roaring through the red light. A few cars skidded and beeped their horns while cursing. Wicker reported, "The Ghost *is* a cop, just like you said. He's your good friend . . . Detective Zaragoza. And he admitted clearly that he is the Ghost."

Cortes wondered how it could be true.

Wicker continued, "Juan Carlo and Gerard were his half-brothers. I didn't get all the details, but he's still in Leo's car right now."

Third Avenue on that side was a wide quiet street with auto shops, gas stations, and industrial supply stores on both sides.

Just upon reaching Hamilton Avenue, the traffic light in front of the overpass turned red.

Wicker stopped at the red light and picked up the radio. "I better call the NYPD for some back up in case we can't find them."

Cortes noticed a little red BMW coming down 3rd Avenue from the opposite way. He didn't get a good look at who was inside the car until it made a left turn onto Hamilton Avenue, right in front of them. Cortes didn't have perfect vision, but he knew what he was seeing. Zaragoza sitting in the passenger seat of Leo's car. "That fucking dirtbag."

Wicker turned to see what Cortes was looking at.

Without warning, he stepped on the gas, running the red light and almost colliding with the cars turning ahead of them.

Cortes felt his body being pushed against the seat he was sitting in as Wicker opened it up.

The little red BMW sped forward, zigzagging between cars.

"Don't lose him."

Wicker asked, "You want to drive?" He continued to barrel forward, through the honking traffic and trying to keep up with the little car.

Cortes picked up the radio to call the NYPD, but when Wicker swerved to avoid hitting a car from a merging street, Cortes dropped the wired microphone. He tried to reach for it, but the movement of the van and the position of him hunched forward, really did a number on his stomach. He lifted his head and tried not to vomit while Wicker continued forward.

Once again, the green steel expressway loomed overhead as they sped past a huge used car lot, a gas station, and rows of decrepit old buildings. Wicker slowed down for a moment and then merged left into more traffic. "He's way up there."

The light turned red. Wicker slowed down but went right through, the little siren still singing.

Cortes reached for the wire and pulled the microphone back up. He gave his DEA identification number and the license plate number of Leo's car. "They're going into the Battery Tunnel."

A man's voice on the radio responded, "Copy that."

Cortes left the radio on so they could hear what was happening in the area.

Agent Wicker kept moving forward as the BQE turned and continued going downtown, leaving them out in the open on a wide four-lane street with a concrete divider in the center.

They slowed down at the tollbooths. Wicker whipped out his badge and ID. "Did NYPD just stop a little red BMW?"

The toll collector responded, "Not since I've been on duty."

"We better not lose them now." Wicker rolled the van forward along with hundreds of other cars, vans, and small trucks.

The hot sun beamed down from above as the street began to descend underground flanked by block walls on both sides. A square beige building housed the two entrances to the tunnel.

Staying in the right lane, they entered the semi-dark tunnel. Soft yellow lights in the metal ceiling above provided enough light to see while the sound of rolling tires echoed off ceramic tile walls on both sides.

A man's voice said something on the radio, but it was mostly static.

Cortes asked, "You hear any of that?"

"Nothing. We gotta get out of this tunnel."

The radio continued to spew static as they moved forward through the tunnel.

Finally out of the tunnel and surrounded by skyscrapers, they veered left and that's when they saw them, turning right onto West Street with the traffic.

Cortes spoke on the radio, "We have them. Coming out of the tunnel. North on West Street."

Traffic ahead let up and the red BMW skidded off.

Wicker stepped on the gas and did a good job of steering the blocky van in and out of the cars.

The light ahead of the BMW turned red. The BMW went through, smashing into a bike messenger who was pedaling at full speed. The bike and its rider flew through the air as cars skidded to a stop and the BMW lost control, spinning out.

The van was right there when Leo's BMW collided with a light post on the corner.

Leo jumped out shooting.

Wicker shot back, easily taking him down.

As Cortes struggled to get out of the van, he noticed Zaragoza getting away by ducking between the stopped cars. "He's getting away!" Cortes moved forward as fast as he could but he knew he would never catch him.

Wicker chased Zaragoza down a narrow street to an open area of grass and benches, The World Trade Center complex. The twin towers shot up into the sky above. The hot sun continued to cook the city while people scurried back and forth between the buildings going about their business.

Cortes was walking fast. There was no way he could run. His gun was in its holster under his windbreaker, which was making him sweat out what little water was left in his body. He was lagging behind, but not so far behind that he couldn't see Wicker chasing Zaragoza through the scattering crowd.

Zaragoza pushed through the people on the way down the escalator and Wicker did the same.

By the time Cortes got to the escalator, he was heaving and hunched over. He stepped on to the moving staircase and let him take him down.

At first, all he could see was people scattering in every direction through the basement shopping mall.

Cortes was worried that he'd lost them, but just then, he spotted them.

Wicker was chasing Zaragoza down a flight of stairs.

Still out of breath, Cortes continued down the escalator to the next floor where there were more stores. Once again, he spotted Wicker chasing Zaragoza through the panicked crowd and toward another flight of stairs.

Whenever his car ended up at the mechanic, Cortes had used the PATH trains to commute between New York and New Jersey, so he knew the station well. And he knew the train station was on the next level, so he saved his energy and continued down on the next escalator, this time walking down instead of just standing there.

Most people knew to stay to the right while the people on the left walked down the escalator, but there was always those one or two people who wanted to stand on the left, even though no one else was in front of them or behind them.

Cortes excused himself and pushed his way by them while going down to the next level where he heard a train's metal wheels screeching against the tracks as it pulled into the station.

Gunshots were already being exchanged before he got there.

Wicker was pinned next to the token booth and didn't have a good shot at Zaragoza who was using a metal newspaper booth as cover.

Cortes ducked down next to the metal escalator and had a perfect shot at Zaragoza, but when he fired, his hands and eyes didn't cooperate with each other. Four shots. All of them missed.

The sound of the train leaving the station below was not enough to mask the sound of Cortes' bullets ricocheting off the metal newspaper booth as Zaragoza moved farther behind it.

Just as Wicker made his move toward the newspaper booth from the other side, a group of commuters began coming up the stairs.

Zaragoza popped out from behind the booth and grabbed a frail woman who instantly began crying. He held his gun to her head. "Drop it!"

Wicker hesitated, but then dropped his gun. Zaragoza fired at Wicker, but Wicker was already on the move.

When Zaragoza let his crying hostage go, Cortes took his shot, but missed again, twice.

Zaragoza jumped over the turnstile, and on his way down the stairs, he pushed his way through the crowd that was coming up.

Wicker was on his way down too, but it was obvious that his size was keeping him from catching Zaragoza who was lean and nimble.

Cortes showed his badge to the token booth clerk who was peeking out his bulletproof window.

The clerk buzzed Cortes in through the handicap entrance.

By the time Cortes was on his way down the stairs, most of the crowd was gone.

At the bottom, another train roared into the station on the opposite side, but the sound of gunfire could still be heard.

Wicker hid behind a wooden bench with very little protection as Zaragoza raced along the platform, firing an occasional wild shot in Wicker's direction.

Cortes let the shells drop from his .38 revolver and then reloaded, one by one. He'd been trained by an old school detective who had spent twenty-five years as a cop in the toughest neighborhoods of Chicago and then joined the DEA. The old cop, now retired, had told him horror stories of cops getting killed because of their guns jamming in the middle of a shootout. Now he was wondering if he'd be killed while reloading.

Zaragoza also was out of ammo.

Wicker bolted as fast as he could while Zaragoza went for another clip.

Cortes was reloaded and happy to see that Wicker was on top of Zaragoza before he could change his magazine. Wicker tackled Zaragoza, taking him down while simultaneously knocking the gun out of his hand and into the train tracks.

They wrestled as Cortes made his way toward them.

Suddenly, Wicker jumped off Zaragoza and tried to pull himself up while holding his hand on his face, which was dripping blood.

Zaragoza quickly jumped to his feet with a knife in his hand. Wicker was on his knees in front of Zaragoza, obviously in shock.

Just as Zaragoza was about to lunge at Wicker with the knife, Cortes fired his gun, three times. And that time, he didn't miss. Zaragoza fell backward, into the train tracks.

Wicker was still on his knees, holding his bleeding face with trembling hands.

Cortes moved toward the tracks. He could see Zaragoza's hand reaching up and grabbing the side of the platform. Cortes could hear the train coming, but there was no way he was going to help Zaragoza.

The train blew its horn and then it appeared, screeching to a stop, sparks flying from the electric tracks.

But it couldn't slow down fast enough.

Just when Zaragoza lifted his head, the train plowed into him.

Cortes felt dizzy and his legs became weak. He felt himself falling and then he lost consciousness.

CHAPTER 79

On Saturday, Angelo picked up his mother at her cousin's house in Long Island and brought her back to Brooklyn where they spent the day shopping on Avenue U. When they got home, she threw away any old food that had been in the refrigerator and then she cooked a pan of chicken Parmigiana.

It was too much food for two people, but Angelo kept his mouth shut. He didn't need to remind her that half of their family was dead. He could always take the leftovers to his friends.

Rather than go to the club, Angelo stayed home that night to keep his mother company. Her friends had asked her to play cards, but she wasn't up to going yet, so they watched whatever she wanted on TV, and Angelo listened to her brag about her cousin's big house in Long Island.

That night, Angelo dreamed of killing Gerard and his wife. He also dreamt of those crying little girls that he'd made orphans. But the dreams didn't upset him anymore. Waking up a few times a night in a cold sweat to murderous nightmares had become a normal part of life.

The next morning, Angelo went downstairs to the kitchen to find it empty. His mother was usually up at the crack of dawn making coffee and preparing what she would be cooking that day, but now the house was silent.

He went back upstairs to his mother's bedroom door, which was closed, and just as he was ready to knock and ask if she's okay, he heard her crying.

Tears filled Angelo's eyes knowing how his mother hurt, but his sorrow was soon interrupted by someone pounding on the front door.

As he hurried down the stairs he exclaimed, "Who the fuck is banging on my door at this time on a Sunday?"

When he opened it, he saw two men in cheap suits who were obviously cops and a tall bearded man with a bandaged face, a short-sleeve plaid shirt, and blue jeans.

One of the suits asked, "Angelo Manigritto?"

"Who wants to know?"

The two cops showed their NYPD badges.

Angelo asked, "What about you? You got no ID, Paul Bunyan?"

The bearded man didn't answer.

The older cop said, "We'd like to ask you a few questions. Do you mind if we come in?"

"Sorry. We don't allow animals in the house."

It was obvious that the younger cop was easily angered and ready to fight. "This mother fucker." He stepped forward. "Who do you think you are?"

The older cop said, "Take it easy. I'll handle this young punk." He then turned back to Angelo and demanded, "Where were you Friday night?"

Angelo put his finger to his temple, pretending to think. "Let's see. Oh yes . . . how can I forget?" He pointed at the young cop and said, "I was busy fucking his mother."

The young cop lunged at Angelo. The older cop put his hands on the young cop, but it was the big bearded man who stopped him.

Angelo invited more trouble. "Let him loose. You think you got a chance against me, you little fucking bitch?"

The older cop commanded, "Stop it. Both of you."

Angelo's mother yelled from somewhere inside the house, "Who's at the door?"

"I got it, Ma." Angelo turned to the older cop and asked, "Why are you here?"

The bearded man said, "You killed Gerard Arroyo and his wife."

Both cops turned their heads to look at the big man.

Angelo responded, "I didn't kill nobody. Maybe one of your crooked fucking cops killed them. It's all over the news what happened yesterday. You think you have a case?" He took a business card from a small stack on the little table by the door. "Call my lawyer."

When he tried to close the door, the tall bearded man put his hand on the door to stop him.

Angelo threatened, "Get the fuck away from my door before I exercise my constitutional right to defend my person and property. Scumbag fucking rats."

The big man stepped back.

Angelo could see the anger on all of their faces as he slammed the door.

His mother was at the bottom of the staircase. "Who was that?"

"No one." Angelo quickly changed the subject to food. "If you don't feel up to it, don't worry about it . . . but, you know . . . I really missed your pancakes."

"You want pancakes?"

"Can we have some eggs with it? I could use the protein."

"Protein . . . protein . . . protein . . . this gym is making you crazy. *Pazzo*."

CHAPTER 80

Agent Cortes was comfortable in his hospital bed watching the Mets lose to the Braves once again when Agent Wicker entered with a bandage on his face.

Cortes asked, "How bad is it?"

"They gave me fifteen stitches. But they said it wasn't that deep so the scarring shouldn't be terrible."

"Don't worry, you'll still be a Don Juan."

When they laughed, Cortes began to cough.

Wicker moved one of the two chairs against the wall closer to the bed and sat down. "I went with NYPD homicide to Angelo Manigritto's house this morning."

"Don't tell me. He gave a full confession."

"Very funny. He gave us his lawyer's business card. He had a stack of them by the door. That smug bastard."

Cortes wanted to change the subject before Wicker was back to wondering how Angelo could have known about Gerard. He said, "I thought you came here to tell me about the Ghost. You going to let me go to my grave without ever knowing?"

Wicker explained, "Well, as you already know, Detective Zaragoza was born and raised in the Bronx and never knew his father . . . but that's not exactly the case. When Zaragoza was three-years-old, his father fled to Puerto Rico after robbing a heroin dealer to pay his gambling debts."

Cortes coughed, then said, "Go ahead. I'm fine."

Wicker continued the story. "It seems that Zaragoza's father returned to New York years later and tried to make amends with his son, who was sixteen at the time and wanted nothing to do with the father who abandoned him. His father left him a letter in a sealed envelope that Zaragoza kept. He finally read the letter seven years later, just after his father died. The letter said that Zaragoza had two half-brothers who were born in Puerto Rico, but have been living in Brooklyn since they were children, Gerard and Juan Carlo Arroyo. None of them had their father's last name. Zaragoza had recently made detective and soon learned that his half-brothers were drug dealers making big money. He arrested them, unofficially, and then told them who he was. That's when they joined forces. Zaragoza killed a few rival gang leaders in Sunset Park and Park Slope to make way for his brothers to take over all their territories. Because no one ever saw or heard anything, the unknown killer was nicknamed *the Ghost.* The gang embraced the rumor of the Ghost and changed their name to match."

Cortes felt satisfied that the Ghost was no longer just a myth and while he was disappointed it turned out to be Detective Zaragoza, he was happy the Ghost was now really a Ghost.

CHAPTER 81

On Monday, Uncle Larry's girlfriend came into Brooklyn to pick up Angelo's mother and then brought her back to Staten Island so they could go shopping together at the mall.

Angelo stayed home and caught a little nap. Every time he heard a loud noise outside, he peeked out the window. Always worried the cops would find a way to tie him to Gerard's murder. Why did they care about a dead drug dealer anyway? Angelo felt as if he had done society a favor. Sure, the wife was innocent, but she could have identified him. Then his mother would have no one.

Later that afternoon, while right in the middle of a somewhat peaceful nap, Angelo was awakened by the phone ringing. He answered it.

It was Frank. "Hey. You wanna go to the gym? Get some blood flowing? Maybe get some aggression out?"

"Yeah. I do. But, not at Big Mike's."

"Don't tell me you're gonna join another gym now."

"I think I have to."

CHAPTER 82

Agent Cortes was out of the hospital on Monday but waited until Tuesday to resume his radiation therapy sessions.

By the time he got home that afternoon, he was once again sick and weak.

When his phone rang, the first thought was that someone was calling him to say that the Ghost was still alive, but he knew that wouldn't be true. He almost ignored it, but at the last minute, he answered.

Agent Wicker asked, "How you feeling, old man?"

"Old man? Who you calling old man?"

They laughed.

Agent Wicker was the closest thing he had to a son.

Wicker said, "You better hurry up and get well. We need you here. The Ghost's turf is up for grabs and it's like the Wild West out there in Brooklyn now. New gangs popping up everywhere."

Cortes had no more desire to fight. He won his battle. And now it was time to leave the rest of the war to the young guys. "You're going to have to do without me. I'm putting in my papers for permanent disability."

"I guess I can't blame you. I'd probably do the same."

"Don't worry. You'll do just fine. You learned from the best."

Agent Wicker chuckled. "Get some rest, old man. I'll stop by and see you during the week. If you need anything, just call me . . . or page me."

CHAPTER 83

Angelo knew that Cara's wake was being held Sunday, Monday, and Tuesday, but he couldn't bring himself to go. Not only did her family blame him for her death, but he blamed himself as well.

On Wednesday morning, he decided to take a chance and go to the burial. Hopefully, if he stayed in the back, no one would notice him.

He already knew that Cara's body would be buried in Queens, so he drove out there early and waited for the family to arrive.

It was almost noon by the time the hearse and the caravan of cars arrived.

Angelo waited in his car far away. Watching everyone gather around the coffin.

He couldn't hear anything, but he had a feeling the priest was saying something similar to what they said at his sister's funeral and his father's funeral.

Finally, after more words and a lot of tears, the crowd dispersed.

Angelo waited until all the cars were gone and the machine finished filling the hole with dirt.

He approached the fresh mound and stood there in his black suit. There were no more tears.

For news, sneak peeks, and free offers, sign up for Phil Nova's newsletter at
http://www.philnova.com

If you enjoyed this book, please leave a review at:
http://www.amazon.com/author/philnova

Books by Phil Nova:

'84 IN BROOKLYN
A novel based on characters from Phil Nova's Joe Martello series.
A dying DEA agent, and the nephew of a mafia capo, are both hunting for the elusive leader of a brutal drug dealing gang.

POLICE BRUTALITY
A novel
An army ranger returns home to find that his wife has become a victim of police brutality.

FOUR KILOS
A novel
Internal Affairs and the mob both suspect a pill-popping homicide detective of theft and murder.

JIHAD ON 34TH STREET
A novel
A Pakistani-American construction worker suspected of being a terrorist eludes a federal agent and tries to find the real terrorists before the feds find him.

JOE MARTELLO
A series of novellas
A lawyer, who was once a New York City cop, helps people in trouble who can't go to the authorities.

Website: http://www.philnova.com
Email: philnova@philnova.com
Facebook: https://www.facebook.com/Phil-Nova-472907306108064/

Also from Five Borough Publishing:
Roman Bernard
Author of fast-paced, suspenseful, science-fiction/fantasy thrillers for adults.
https://www.amazon.com/author/romanbernard

www.ingramcontent.com/pod-product-compliance
Lightning Source LLC
LaVergne TN
LVHW090940080826
845145LV00003B/823

* 9 7 8 0 5 7 8 7 2 3 9 7 6 *